Lines of Truth and Conversation

Lines of Truth

JOAN ALEXANDER

and Conversation

The Porcupine's Quill

Library and Archives Canada Cataloguing in Publication

Alexander, Joan, 1954–

Lines of truth and conversation / Joan Alexander.

Short Stories.

ISBN 0-88984-271-X

I. Title.

PS8601.L428L56 2005   C813'.6   C2005-900791-5

1   2   3   4   •   07   06   05

Published by The Porcupine's Quill,
68 Main Street, Erin, Ontario N0B 1T0.
www.sentex.net/~pql

Readied for the press by John Metcalf; copy edited by Doris Cowan.

This is a work of fiction. Names, characters, and incidents are the
product of the author's imagination, and any
resemblance to actual persons or events is entirely coincidental.

Represented in Canada by the Literary Press Group.
Trade orders are available from University of Toronto Press.

We acknowledge the support of the Ontario Arts Council
and the Canada Council for the Arts for our publishing program.
The financial support of the Government of Canada
through the Book Publishing Industry Development Program
is also gratefully acknowledged. Thanks, also
to the Government of Ontario through the Ontario
Media Development Corporation's Ontario Book Initiative.

**Canada Council
for the Arts**

**Conseil des Arts
du Canada**

ONTARIO ARTS COUNCIL
CONSEIL DES ARTS DE L'ONTARIO

For Stan,
Nathan and Elie

They have been at a great feast of languages, and stolen the scraps.
– Shakespeare, *Love's Labour's Lost*

Table of Contents

Love Junk

When Patti's yoga teacher said, Come home to the spirit of wholeness, Patti thought, Come home to adultery, that's more like it. Her heart was full of Dr David Olive, who lay beside her, deep into his spinal twist. Even though her consciousness was supposed to be centred inward, Patti couldn't help but watch the way Dr Olive rolled over into the fetal position and how he drew his arms up to his handsome head and rubbed his hands over his face like an infant. As Dr Olive sat up, he twisted his legs into the full-lotus pretzel of a guru, and placed his hands open on his knees in the position of reception. On his left wrist was a leather strap with a bead of coral blue. His wedding ring, a thin gold band, was much like the one Patti had taken off several years before when she and Barry had been incessantly fighting. The yoga teacher had dark hair roiling back from her forehead. She said, 'Breathe in peace, breathe out peace,' and Patti breathed in the beauty of Dr David Olive, his tie-dyed pants and clean, beautiful toes. The chanting of *om* lingered in the room. I want to make love to Dr Olive, Patti breathed in, I'm a flower. And he is a vision of pulchritude.

Dr Olive was waiting for her by the elevators. He asked if she would read a letter he had written to her three weeks ago after they had first met.

'I hope you'll trust me,' Dr Olive said.

'Why wouldn't I?' She couldn't believe she was talking to him.

'I've carried this letter everywhere.' His blue eyes were large and pleading, his lips trembled as he spoke. 'To yoga, to volleyball, to the hospital. I was just waiting for an opportunity to give it to you.'

Patti was embarrassed by his candour in front of the other students milling in the hallway. She reached out her hand in a gesture that she hoped was bold, but casual. 'I could use a pick-me-up,' she said.

Her name was scrawled across the thick envelope in large black letters: PATTI. Above the double T's was a stamp of two yellow warblers from the World Wildlife Fund.

It was a cold spring evening in early April. Out on the street rain was falling, dark and heavy. Patti stopped to buy a pack of cigarettes, although she hadn't smoked since her youngest boy, Jack, was born twelve years ago. Then she ducked into a café up the block where she sat down toward the back of the crowded room and ordered a cup of tea. She carefully settled herself, lit a cigarette, and opened the envelope. It was a long letter, typed in a small font on legal size paper. Patti began to read.

April 4, 1998

Dear Patti,

In the fall of 1987, I arrived on the mysterious, sea-swept German island of Sylt. In this place of sleepless oceans and endless rows of dunes, I entered one of the brief monastic pauses of my life, finding, as I often do, the Lush in the Desolate.

Why is he telling me this? Patti asked herself. Still, her attention did not waver. As she read on, she seriously tried to maintain the hope that traces of real brilliance would soon be revealed.

I believe in speaking and writing from a base of knowledge. My major area of expertise is the culture of the First World War as embodied in the poets of this era. I have seen a lot of the world, from Norway to Peru, but I do not travel well alone, especially as a non-smoker. (I quit six years ago, and have a highly addictive personality. Everyone smokes in Europe. Especially in France.)

With satisfaction Patti inhaled deeply. Which First World War poets? she wondered. Never mind, she thought. What a passport! Maybe this was a travel invitation.

A long time ago I wanted a great deal from life. I was a little different and a little shy. There were times in my twenties when I'd actually be in tears, because I could not find the power of speech, even
though I possessed the words I wanted to say in my mind. I'd meet
people in bars and get their addresses instead of their telephone
numbers and then send them letters. When I relied on the written
sentence, I could overlook the everyday emotions that form the
backbone of life, and offer, in their place, highly charged and erotic
prose.

Patti reread this passage. The idea that he could be repeating an
old pattern quickly became muddled up in the following description
of his short, but exhilarating stint as a novelist.

The period began during my internship and carried through the
first years of my work. Even during some traditional psychother-
apy, I could never understand how the forces awakened within me.
There were times when I felt in touch with a bigger universe, with
the truths that link centuries over great expanses of time.

Patti paused to ask herself if she had ever felt the way Dr Olive
had, but she could hardly formulate a question beyond her plans for
Saturday night. She checked her watch to see how she was doing for
time. It wasn't every day that she received such a letter. She asked the
waitress to bring her some more hot water.

By now it seemed to Patti that Dr David Olive went on at too great
length about almost everything. His struggle with Judaism, his
mother's desire that he pursue a career in music ('I won a little junior
notoriety playing piano in my late adolescence'), and his eventual
marriage, ten years ago, at the age of thirty, to his wife, Ashley. 'Time
to become soulfully bourgeois,' he wrote.

Finally Patti struck on a paragraph about her.

During the discussion class three weeks ago, I first had the liberating sense that beside me was a soul-mate. I linked the exact *knowing* to the moment when you uttered *gnosticism* in a sentence, as if it were just another word like dog, or ball, or spaghetti. When you mentioned your love of poetry, I knew I must write to you, even though this territory must be, no doubt, highly personal.

I intrigue him, Patti thought.
Also, there was this:

I am not oppressed by the need to be known; I endure the need for patience and learn to find meaning in the enduring. What I possibly have to offer you is important enough, I feel, to break taboo, while respecting who you are, your marriage, children, and the important work you are doing at the women's shelter.

And this was good too, in spite of the long wait.

The Patti-ness and Patti-feelings I experience add to the bloom of my classes. Already there is greater fullness to this moment. You have aroused magic within me. Because of my comfort in your presence, I seek to touch the special part of you that connects to the special part of me.

I do not want to vanish into the mist of those-never-known.

Your fellow yogi,

David

Next to his phone number and e-mail address, there were also a few lines that Patti could not ignore:

1.) Have you ever corresponded with a stranger?; and 2.) Over a year ago I already dealt with my sexual attraction to another student in the class.

Patti stubbed out her third cigarette, Anna Karenina and Madame Bovary in one forty-three-year-old Patti-body. Nonetheless, as she walked through the rain to the bus stop, she was also suffused with a great Patti-happiness.

On the bus ride home, she recollected their first meeting in the yoga studio.

'What brings you here?' he had asked. 'Are you on a spiritual path?'

'I'm Jewish,' she said. 'Not a Jew in the lotus. I'm not on a mystical route.'

'Just quiet exercise?'

'My kids drive me crazy. They're bright and loving, but more than active. They make me nervous. The demands never end.'

She remembered telling him about her job at the shelter. 'I must see a rapist at least once a week.' My God, he'd looked interested in what she had to say. His head tilted towards her. What a handsome, no, a gorgeous man, she couldn't stop looking at his face. And such a soft voice.

'I don't want to take Prozac,' she recalled saying. 'I'm not against it. But the side effects. Don't you agree?'

'By all means. Take care of yourself. You deserve it.'

'Don't we all? Don't we all?'

Dear God, he was dazzling, in truly fine physical shape, and a thick head of hair.

'Does your husband come to yoga?' he had asked.

'No. He plays golf in the summer. Sometimes a little tennis.' She had pointed to her knees. 'Trouble with arthritis.'

Then he must have known. She was not available.

'I've been to India,' he said. 'The *sous-continent sans espoir*. And to Israel, have you?'

'To Israel, yes. But not to India.'

'When? What year?'

'Two years in Tel Aviv helping to establish a centre for battered women.'

A *landtsman*, Patti thought, we're from the same tribe. What a coming together. *Shalom*. Really *shalom*.

'Do you have children?' she asked.

'No. It wasn't planned that way. But I understand a mother's love, a parent's grief. I witnessed a crib death.' He paused. 'The only time I've counselled prayer.'

A kind man, a gentle man. And a doctor, a triage physician. Yet so even, so peaceful, so calm in his meditative pose.

'What a strenuous job,' she had said.

'Ten-hour shifts. It can be gruelling. There's a great need for patience. To relax I like to get out on the lake in my canoe … and read Thoreau. That's how I escape on a Saturday afternoon.'

I love canoes, thought Patti. I love lakes and Thoreau and Saturday afternoons. Oh, why hadn't she met him eighteen years before instead of stepping like a fool into her marriage with … with Barry!

'For unconditional love, I just look into the eyes of my dog,' he said.

How simple yet how profound. How absolutely profound. Just stare into your dog's eyes, even though you have a hundred things to do. Why hadn't she ever thought of that? When the house was in total chaos, she could just take the dog's head in her hands and stare into his eyes. What good and charming advice.

Surely they were meant for each other. This Dr Olive was lovely, and dear too. A gift from heaven. What else could you call such an angel?

So excited had Patti been by their conversation that she had tripped on her way to the bathroom, almost toppling over the yoga teacher who was talking with another student about purity.

The dog jumped up on Patti when she walked through the door. The boys, Jack and Noah, were arguing over Nintendo in the living room. The windows were closed and the air was heavy with the smell of fried food. In the kitchen, Barry was hunched over a plate of chicken and corn.

'You look like Quasimodo,' Patti said. 'Wipe your face and hands.' She handed him a napkin.

'Om baa nama,' Noah said, wandering in. 'I told my friends how you sit and say "Om baa nama" for hours and hours.'

'That's not true. That's not what I say.'

'Everyone was laughing. It's so lame.' Noah swung his arm around Patti's neck.

'Om baa nama,' sang Jack, following his brother.

'Om baa nama,' sang Noah.

The letter from David Olive made great girlfriend talk.

After dinner Patti went over to Lynn, who lived across the street. Upstairs in Lynn's bedroom, they sat cross-legged on the end of the bed. Lynn looked like a teenager. She wore her daughter's overalls and her hair was long and curly.

'The fact is that you're both married,' Lynn said. She was holding the letter. 'I want to be honest. Most of this is about him. There's very little about you. Why didn't he just ask you out for coffee?'

'If he likes the way I say *gnosticism*,' said Patti, 'he should hear me say *kabbalah*.'

'You saw what cheating did to me,' said Lynn. She was raising three kids on her own.

'I haven't forgotten.'

'What does his wife do?'

'I think she's an accountant. And they don't have children.'

'They're DINKS. Double Income No Kids. They must have money.'

'Dr Olive converted my name to a -ness. Maybe he's falling in love with me.'

'It's tax season,' Lynn said. 'His wife's busy. April is her month.'

Before she went to bed, Patti closed her bedroom door and called her friend Ann-Marie, in Florida. Ann-Marie worked as a psychologist in a men's prison.

'It means you can still tingle,' said Ann-Marie. 'Go on, grab for happiness.'

'I don't think Barry would be very happy to hear I'm tingling.'

'You're going to stay with someone who drags his knuckles on the ground for the sake of morality? You'd rather live with a grunter? What does this Dr Olive look like?'

'He's amazing. Almost perfect. A real Adonis.'

Ann-Marie said, 'Today a guy who pistol-whipped his wife offered to marry me when he gets out of detox. Are you sure this Dr Olive isn't a caveman?'

'I haven't felt this way in years.'

'So you're not sure.'

'His bones haven't been tested.'

'You'd better be sure. Tingles or stupidity. I don't think I've missed an option.'

Patti read the letter over and over again. She carried it with her wherever she went. She struggled with the implications of whatever it was Dr David Olive had been trying to say. Who cared how he wrote it? He had said it, hadn't he, when all along, she had thought she was invisible.

It was a cold spring. But the daffodils were out, the hyacinths and tulips were in bloom. Patti tried to see a face in every pansy, the way she had when she was a girl.

April became a difficult month for Barry. At a Chinese restaurant Patti watched him eat. She wasn't hungry.

'I thought the chicken and broccoli was pretty good.' Barry said. He was licking plum sauce off his fingers. 'How about you?'

'Do you have to be so primitive? You eat like a heathen.'

'What's with you, Patti? You used to like this place.'

'I'm not interested in food.'

'What then?' Barry caught her hand. 'I had a nocturnal emission last night.'

'Is that some universal law of gravitation?'

'It means I'm interested.'

Patti broke open her fortune cookie.

'What's it say?' he asked.

'"A merry heart maketh a cheerful countenance."'

'That's a joke,' Barry said. 'You look pretty glum.'

'No, you're a joke. The boys are a joke, the house is a joke, my job is a joke.'

'The dog is a joke,' Barry kept going.

'No,' said Patti seriously. 'The dog is not a joke. Only you would never understand that, would you? Because you're dense and insensitive and you never look into his eyes.'

'Who says I don't? I like the dog.'

As soon as they were in bed, Barry started clicking in the back of his throat. 'Could you stop that?' said Patti.

'Stop what?'

'That infernal clicking.'

'I've clicked my whole life. This is nothing new.'

'Why don't you see a doctor? I think there's a laser to burn the epiglottis.'

'What are you talking about? I'm not going to burn my throat.' Barry rolled over and began to click again.

She nudged him with her elbow. 'You're keeping me awake.'

'Patti! What are you starting?'

She imitated the clicking, a scratching sound from deep in the larynx. 'How would you like it? Every night, year after year. It's impossible to sleep. You'd leave me.'

'I doubt it. Just put a pillow over your head.'

It was not out of a sense of duty that Patti showed up at yoga class the following day. She was not looking for tranquility. You must draw inspiration from the syllabus of love inside you, said the yoga teacher. Each cell, intelligent and listening, is programmed for love. After class Dr Olive offered to walk Patti to the bus.

'Does your wife know you wrote me such a letter?' she said.

'I left it on the kitchen table.' He was making an effort to keep up with Patti. It was clear that walking wasn't his activity. 'I don't like secrets.'

'Do you have an open marriage?'

'Not sexually. I've been very loyal to Ashley.'

'I don't get it. Is there another kind of open marriage? Or are you impotent?' How direct she was becoming. What things she was suddenly able to say! Let him think what he wants, she thought. Let him think Patti has a Patti-sense of humour.

Dr Olive smiled. 'That's never been a problem. Ashley knows the trick.'

'I'm flabbergasted,' she said. 'I haven't received a letter like this in twenty years. I was just marching along to middle age.' They stopped in front of an antique store. Rays of green, yellow and red refracted off the objects of coloured glass in the window. They sat down on painted blue wooden steps.

'What is it you really want from me?' Patti said. She took a water bottle from her canvas satchel.

'That's easy. I want a friend. I know that sounds like some adolescent mantra.'

The limbs of budding trees formed a crown around Dr Olive's head. He spoke about Siegfried Sassoon and the south of Spain and his recent readings on the age of Kaliyuga. These were topics that she and Barry would never discuss.

Then Dr Olive said, 'Those are very nice leggings you're wearing. I like the stripes.'

'Whew,' said Patti. She shielded her eyes from the sun. 'Don't you know anything at all about the seduction of attention?'

'I know it makes me happy to be talking to you. It's a happy ending.'

'Ending?' Patti was confused again. 'I thought this was the beginning.'

That night Patti and Barry watched *60 Minutes*. Patti tried to nestle close to him at precisely the same instant Barry reached out for a bottle of Coke. His arm sliced across her neck.

'Ow!'

'What are you trying to do?' He got up to put popcorn into the microwave.

'I was trying to be friendly.'

'Do you want a tea?' Barry called from the kitchen. 'I'll make you a tea.'

After everyone was asleep, Patti e-mailed Dr Olive for the first time. The bleeping and static of the modem were raucous, reverberating through the quiet house.

Subject: Pen Pals

April 17, 1998

Dear D.,

I'm a fool to write you. I know it. You make me feel blurry. Absolutely blurry. This is not correspondence with a stranger. To me it's playing with fire. You must be cut off from your feelings, in spite of your sensitivity, which I believe is real. How do you march along your merry way like a boy would?

Did my energy bring you alive?

P.

P.S. Don't leave my e-mails on the kitchen table, or I'll hate you. Call it a secret or respecting my privacy. You said you had something to offer me.

Patti pressed the SEND button. The whole thing was terribly quick. She was glad she had decided not to include the Theodore Roethke poem, 'Her Reticence', which contained an image of a disembodied hand. The following day Patti heard back.

Subject: I'm An Adult Now!

April 18, 1998

Dear Patti,

I very much do want to respond. I watched a show last night about Jack Kerouac's 63 days alone on Desolation Peak; he went up to find a vision and came down a broken man.

You pushed me away at the bus station. I actually stood at the bottom of the stairs for a few minutes, considered ascending and trying to find a way for us to part on a better note. Patti, you have no idea how comforting it is for me to be able to reach you.

I have desired from the outset to cultivate a friendship (albeit a meaningful and confusing one, with shades and tones and undercurrents). I offer you a level playing field in giving and receiving.

What in the hell was he talking about? But she didn't care. He was willing to ascend stairs, something Barry would never do even if she paid him. This Ashley was a lucky girl. And a DINK to boot.

Patti waded on.

And so, Patti, if you are playing with fire, try to see fire in its many incarnations, as holy and blessed. And yes, the one fact that never changes, fire burns. And burns heal. As an emergency room physician, I know that only the deepest burns scar.

While I was writing and becoming a doctor, drugs sustained and fulfilled curiosity (although the quality fell off in intensity after a few years).

Have you ever done chemicals?

David

P.S. Please be assured that your correspondence will be guarded in a sacred fashion.

P.P.S. Useful details. It's okay to call here if you want to. Ashley would be fine, but she isn't in the house between 8 am and 11 pm until the end of the month. Cheers.

Patti read Dr Olive's message over twice and then wrote back:

Subject: Too Much Talk

Dear D.,

I've talked to my friends for days about this. About my feelings for you. I've done more talking than I'm used to. Maybe we can be friends. Whatever that means.

P.

P.S. I once did acid in a swimming pool.
P.P.S. Forget the sacred. Just respect my privacy.

The fantasies were unbelievable. Chest kisses, arm kisses, back-of-the-knee kisses, hair kisses, a thousand-thousand kisses, the whole nine yards of kisses, mouth to mouth. Every day Patti passed a hundred strangers, a hundred faces on the street, but all she could think of was Dr David Olive. Her dreams were filled with words and numbers, a gematria of collected poems and letters exchanged.

At home Patti was flighty. She argued and found fault with the children and Barry. To the children, she said things like 'Make it snappy' and 'I haven't time for shenanigans'. She shrank Barry's favourite sweatshirt in the dryer. At work, she was efficient, but curt. Everyone will think I'm unstable, she thought. I am unstable.

One morning she tried to relocate her old therapist by calling 411. She listened to 'Building a Mystery' over and over and over again. She listened to it six times in a row, then thirty-six times in a row, then seventy-two times in a row.

Jack said, 'Mom really likes that song.'

'Mom,' Noah said, 'it's over with that song. Quit. Give it up. Move on.'

'Let us listen to our music,' Jack said. 'I want to hear "Love Junk".'

'Yeah, Mom,' said Noah. '"Pursuit of Happiness".'

Patti imagined Dr David Olive growing older, greyer, his eyes still bright and twinkling behind his wire-rim glasses. He became mild-mannered and generous with her boys, who were now in their twenties and only gambolling in on an occasional weekend home from college.

And Patti had new pages to pore over. E-mails were flowing back and forth like bees transporting pollen. Patti took the accumulating correspondence over to Lynn. 'Look, I can't finish all of this,' Lynn said. She dropped the pages down on the bed. 'Does this guy have any sense of humour? Why don't you make love with your husband? Barry can be funny.'

'But Barry would never ascend stairs.'

'Tell me about it. My husband was ascending stairs all over this city.'

Ann-Marie called to see how things were going.

'It doesn't mean I don't love Barry and the boys,' Patti said. 'This is something quite separate. More like the way I'm able to love both my children at once.' Then Patti read Ann-Marie certain favourite paragraphs.

'It's a dilemma,' Ann-Marie said. 'Like hormones.'

'The problem here is that I'm envisioning.'

'You sound like a jailbird. Wide open possibilities. Does Dr Olive feel the same?'

'I don't know.'

'Be careful, Patti. Tingles is one thing, stupidity another.'

'And behind bars?'

'It's safe.'

And then finally the weather was glorious. Spring. Warm, hot spring. For Patti, the pavement came alive. The breeze filled her heart. On a

Thursday, when she hoped she would see Dr Olive, she fasted all day. I'm in love with someone, she sighed. I'm in love.

Again Dr Olive waited for her after class. They were sitting on a park bench.

'I've been married eighteen years,' said Patti. 'None of this open stuff. When I say married, I mean really married.'

'Yes,' he said. 'I think I understand.'

'Like right now,' Patti blurted, 'I want to push you into that stairwell.' Dr Olive looked to where Patti pointed across the busy street.

'That particular stairwell?'

'You know what I mean.'

'I'm flattered.'

'You should be.'

He smiled.

'I'm serious,' she said, sticking up for herself.

'Doesn't it say something in the Bible about loyalty to your wife?' he asked.

'What?'

'I thought we were going to discuss matters of Jewish renewal,' he said. 'I thought you represented my quest for connectedness to the community.'

'You're kidding,' said Patti.

'Aren't you the one who's always quoting the Rabbi of Lvov? The Rabbi of Bialystok? The Baal Shem Tov?'

'Who?' Patti said. 'When did I talk about them?'

'But I don't even know you.'

Okay, thought Patti, crushed, but still capable of standing.

'It would be so easy if I touched your shoulders,' Dr Olive said.

'Stop.'

He said, 'I'd be so torn between wanting to give you pleasure and my own conscience.'

'Please. Don't you know your effect on people?' Patti stood to go.

'Patti, what's going to become of us?' Dr Olive reached out his arms like long black shadows. 'A hug?'

Patti looked at him with indignation, turned, and walked away.

That night Barry came into the bedroom. She pretended to read.

'Did you like those perogies I made for dinner?' he said, chucking her under the chin. 'Pretty good, eh? I bought them ready-made.'

Lynn said, 'If you want an affair, pick out someone who's normal. That guy was weird from the start. He couldn't give you a straight answer if you asked him the time.'

Ann-Marie said, 'When you see him with his wife, just laugh. Laugh out loud when you see him with his wife.'

All night Patti cried. And while she was crying, she thought about what she, Patti, knew about the Rabbi of Bialystok, or was it the Rabbi of Lvov, she didn't remember. Before he became a great man, a holy man and a leader to his people, when he was young and employed as a dishwasher in a poor village inn, he had said holiness was nothing more than making sure that the pots and pans stayed clean.

At the women's shelter the next morning Patti found Amelia. Amelia was a lesbian, intolerant of straight men. She worked the night shift. Her hair was clipped short, and a tattoo of a rattlesnake coiled its way around her right shoulder.

'We need the poetry,' Amelia said like a Marine. 'Have you been collecting the poetry? Are you doing anything at all about poetry night?'

'I'll start,' said Patti.

'These women need to be taken to the opera, to the ballet, to the theatre. Everyone is totally bored out of their mind.'

'Okay,' said Patti.

Amelia thrust the morning paper at Patti. 'Funding cuts. Welfare reform. We need to raise money. And soon.'

'From poetry night?'

'I had five women with seven kids between them come in last night. That's twelve in the meeting room that need to be fed.'

'Did the children have breakfast?' But her voice quavered.

Amelia stared at Patti. 'You look like shit,' she said. 'Dump that joker. Did you tell him to start using his dick as well as his typewriter?'

'Not in so many words.'

'You should have.'

E-mails not sent.

Subject: Love Junk

Hey, Lovejunk. What happened to soul-mates and planted silences and Jack Kerouac and two yellow warblers, no matter what, no matter why? I want to rip your skin off, sear your eyeballs wide open, step on your beautiful toes. If you write back, don't tell me about your trip to Lithuania in search of your roots. I'm not your mother the Litvak! Tell me what you feel.

P.

Reason not sent: He'll know he hurt me.

Subject: Paris

Meet me in Paris this summer while my boys are at camp. We'll stay in bed for a week. Forget the Louvre. Forget the Pompidou. Forget Notre Dame!

Patti

Reason not sent: I hate to fly.

Subject: *Intermezzo*

Did you ever see the film *Intermezzo* with Ingrid Bergman and Leslie Howard? It's about a concert violinist and his little girl's piano teacher. They have a passionate love affair even though they finally decide they can't build their new found happiness on the suffering of others. He returns to his family in Sweden and she gets a scholarship in France. It's a great movie. She has to leave him without saying goodbye because they really do love each other. Write back if you have the time.

Patti

Reason not sent: Sad ending

Subject: DINK Vacations

What do DINKS do when they need to get away? A three day bike trip, a hot springs spa just outside the city, or a downtown hotel weekend, continental breakfast inclusive, free VCR??????

Reason not sent: seems like a lightbulb joke.

Subject: Complications

D.,

Is this more complicated than I think? Are you gay?

P.

Reason not sent: none of my business.

Subject: The Yoga Mistress

David, I can't help myself. I don't want to help myself.

Signed, Scarlet Patti

Reason not sent: apparent dissolution.

Thank goodness it was May. Patti stopped going to yoga.

Baseball and carpooling and standing in line for junk food took over. Special orders of pickles and extra mustard and French fries with gravy. 'Great pitch, Noah!' Patti shouted out to the mound. She went shopping and bought a new pair of sunglasses and a belt with a buckle that was way too big for her jeans. She planted impatiens, sent an overdue birthday card, gave charitable donations over the phone and went to the library to take out books of poetry.

Patti raked the front garden before she went to work. She cleared the dead grass, put down fertilizer, and sowed new seed. She took Jack to buy three new goldfish, which he named for the flowers of spring, Geranium, Marigold and Dusty Miller. When she went grocery shopping, she did not buy olives. If someone mentioned the name, David, a boy on the team, a kid in a class, Patti said 'Who?' and turned the other way.

Patti told herself she was happy and content, and that Dr David Olive, expert on fractures and lacerations, was a thing of the past.

The clicking in the back of Barry's throat before he fell asleep became dearer. She put her arm around him one night; he was warm and familiar. 'I'm suddenly interested in physics,' she said and they made love. Afterwards, he said sleepily, 'I love you, Patti. I think you're pretty. You're my popsicle.'

Then once, in the middle of the night, Patti awoke to find Barry inside her, heavy and groaning, his breath hard upon her shoulder, cumbersome and suffocating.

'What are you doing?' she said and pushed him away.

'Oh, c'mon.'

'Hello, remember me?'

'It was good, Patti.' He was happy and excited. 'Do I need an appointment?'

'You're revolting.'

She got out of bed and went down to the kitchen. Barry was not even human, she thought. He was disgusting, a horror, a thing. He knew nothing about women. Or love. Or lovemaking. He did not ascend stairs. If only she could get away from him. But how? She went out into the garden with her cigarettes and wine in a jelly jar. She brought a paperback copy of Yeats's poems. All the lights in the neighbourhood were out. The moon was hidden. She smoked her cigarettes and put the ashes in a clay pot. She read Yeats by the dinky yard light. The cat yawned and the dog went to bed, tired of waiting for bread ends.

If only she didn't want a souvenir. If only there were a boulevard, a dark café, a lonely cinema, a crowded street where she could hang on to the hope of running into Dr Olive. Why had she ever given him up? She came indoors and e-mailed him three stanzas from 'The Phases of the Moon'.

ROBARTES

All thought becomes an image and the soul
Becomes a body: that body and that soul
Too perfect at the full to lie in a cradle,
Too lonely for the traffic of the world:
Body and soul cast out and away
Beyond the visible world.

AHERNE

All dreams of the soul
End in a beautiful man's or woman's body.

ROBARTES

Have you not always known it?

A week later he called her. He said he was at the hospital.
'I'm poetry dyslexic,' Dr Olive began.
'Don't make me explain. It was a complete aberration.'
'My life is madness.'
'I had trouble saying goodbye,' said Patti.
'Was burning up with fever all last week.'

He was quiet. She waited. She'd been burning too.

'Who knows?' he said. 'We may end up together.'

'What are you saying?'

'You have more to lose than I do.'

'That's right,' Patti said. 'Don't take down the barbed wire. Put a gunner on the watchtower. Gimme a fence a hundred yards high.'

'It's not impossible. Only a fool confuses fear with integrity.' He paused. 'Maybe not.'

'What's that supposed to mean? Maybe-maybe-not. You drive me crazy.'

'I still know so little about you.'

'That seems vaguely beside the point. You may have taken the high road. But I fell bleeding on the pavement.'

'I'm thinking of you, Patti. Without even trying.'

Patti returned to yoga.

Dr Olive stood in a halo of golden-pink light streaming through the window blinds. Others stood dully around him nibbling oranges.

He was holding a cup of steamy herbal tea. Unnoticed, Patti watched his beautiful figure from the doorway of the waiting area.

'Ashley!' Dr Olive trumpeted. Patti saw him cross the room to where a woman was unlacing her sandals. She stood to greet him. This Ashley was full-bodied and swarthy, much fleshier than Patti. And much larger breasts. The couple began to talk. Instead of 'canoe' or 'lake', Patti distinctly heard Dr Olive say 'at the shopping mall'. Then the yoga teacher came over to them.

'Did you see we signed up for the workshop?' Dr Olive said.

'Which one?' asked the yoga teacher.

'On tantric sex.'

Patti considered leaving. But when the door opened, and the previous class, a group of flamenco dancers, came out, Patti trotted in and set up at the back of the room. Dr Olive pulled his yoga mat next to Ashley at the front. He looked around the studio, now filling up with students, and gave Patti a friendly little wave.

What an asshole, she thought.

During the first part of the class, Patti tried feeling sorry for Ashley, but she couldn't concentrate on pity in spite of her breath awareness. Ashley did all the yoga moves. Married to him? She'd need to be as double-jointed as a carnival freak. Who cared?

'Sink into formlessness,' said the yoga teacher. 'Let substance dissolve.'

There she is, thought Patti. His wifeness of a wife. I'd better think fast. She remembered how her friends had warned that fixations can go on and on. Patti felt sick and hungry. God, I have the greatest friends, she thought. They understood all along. Why would I think 'level playing field' and 'mysterious island' meant love? Knock. Knock. Anybody home? Triple quadruple consummate infinite fool! She could kick herself.

'Arms up,' said the yoga teacher. 'Open the chest. Open the shoulders. Open the heart. Yoga mudra, the posture of forgiveness. The symbol of yoga.'

Patti lay on her back in the corpse pose.

'Go inside,' said the yoga teacher. 'Keep your eyes closed.'

Patti opened her eyes.

'We are all one,' the yoga teacher said.

Not entirely, Patti said to herself. I'm going to stop fasting and eat a roast beef sandwich.

She wasn't surprised when this letter came by e-mail.

Subject: Discontinuities

May 28, 1998

Dear Patti,

I want to start by a touch that softly grazes the outermost cells on the back of your neck. I close my eyes and imagine us somewhere in the high mountains of Tibet, inches from contact, beyond the next crest of snow-peaked daggers, slashing Kaliyuga's thin sky.

Close to each other, to Nature, to God and union. Let's stay here for a few minutes before we return to our other lives ...

I cannot believe this lull is a permanent thing. I call it a discontinuity and not a parting because this is the way I try to see life in all its progressions.

David

The sky was clearing overhead. On a Monday afternoon Patti called Dr Olive at his home. She stood on her back porch holding the portable phone.

'I thought I'd go straight to the source,' she said when he answered.

'You caught me doing something Zen,' Dr Olive said. 'I'm cooking my dog's food.' He sounded happy to hear from her.

'Listen,' she started to say.

'Patti,' he interrupted, 'Ashley's glad my feelings are reciprocated.'

'You told her?'

He paused. 'Yes. She understands passion.'

'Does she understand "I want to graze the outermost cells on the back of your neck"?'

'I write in a dream.'

'Who cares?' Patti said. 'You're a jerk. Pathetically vain and self-absorbed.'

'I can't help it. I like you. You make me feel special.'

'Kaliyuga mountain one minute and goodbye ditch the next.'

Patti roared into the phone receiver. His dog started barking. Patti thought maybe Dr Olive was having fun.

'You fucking fuck,' she said.

'I can go away.'

'Not far enough. Is your travel agent booking the moon?'

'I can't offer immunity,' he said.

'What? No vaccine? It's okay. I don't have the virus.'

Patti was sorting laundry in the basement. I'd rather do laundry, she thought. At least with laundry, you can separate light from dark. You've got a pair of jeans, a black T-shirt, a navy sweatshirt. You put those all in the dark pile. A white blouse goes in whites. White underwear and white socks stay together. It's true you have to watch out for delicates. But it's not that complicated.

Should she tell Barry? He'd make a joke and wave her aside. Nothing happened, he would say, it was nothing. So what.

Patti loaded the washing machine and gazed into its sudsy vortex.

The front door banged shut. Barry and the boys were home.

'Mom!' Jack screamed. 'Mom! I hit a line drive off Mikey Levin's fastball.'

'Right up third base in the bottom of the ninth,' Barry called down. 'It was beautiful.'

'We won,' Noah yelled happily.

Patti sighed. She considered what was lost. That was beauty too.

She turned off the light in the laundry room.

Sun was pouring in through the side door. A pool of rainbow-coloured light lay on the carpet. Patti walked through it and ascended the stairs.

Snap

In 1962, not long after the Cuban missile crisis, when I was eight years old, my father married for the second time. My brother, Teddy, and Ruby, Jill's daughter, were the only guests in attendance, besides me. The wedding took place in a rabbi's study where the three of us children sat like separate stars at various points in the sky. During the ceremony, I cleaned out a little patent leather purse with a metal clasp that my grandmother had given me to carry my things in – a tissue, a comb and a bow for my hair. *Snap.* I opened the purse and took out the things, one at a time. A tissue, a comb, a bow for my hair, and I laid them out on my lap or next to me on an empty chair, and then, after a moment's rearrangement, I put them all back, one by one, and shut the purse. *Snap.* When the ceremony was over, and everyone had told me how bothersome the snapping sound had been and what a nuisance I was, my brother and I were taken home to Jill's apartment.

Jill's apartment was on the south side of Chicago, near Jeffrey Boulevard and 72nd Place, a spacious flat, light and airy, on the first floor of a greystone building with three bedrooms and a back porch. It was stylish. Couches as shapely and sleek as greyhounds, a piano in the front window, visible from the street, and a coffee table made of glass. The dining-room set was made of burnished teak whereas my grandmother had a heavy dark mahogany table and chairs in the dining room of her apartment on Ridgeland Avenue. My father and I had been living with her for the last four years, ever since my parents' divorce.

At Jill's my brother was given the spare room across from the kitchen and I was put on the porch in back of Ruby's room. Now, of course, I would appreciate a windowed room with plenty of light streaming in. But it was December and the room was grey and cold in spite of the hot water radiator sputtering on the back wall. I must have felt the set-up was unfair, including the linoleum floor; except for the kitchen, the rest of the apartment was carpeted in a light beige broadloom. Every room, it seemed to me, had matching furniture except mine. I had been given a laminated dresser whose drawers hardly closed and a folding cot whose exposed metal frame and thin green blanket gave the room a stark and penal appearance. Nevertheless, I was excited to be in the same apartment as a piano.

I had brought with me a small suitcase of clothes that my grandmother helped me to pack, my hamster's cage, and my hamster, Noreen. I put Noreen's cage on the dresser. She was nosing about in her shavings; she only ran around on her wheel at night. I don't remember changing into pyjamas; I don't remember getting undressed. My party clothes were hand-me-downs from Ruby and had been brought up from the basement where the clothes she had outgrown were packed and stored in boxes, waiting to be given away to charity, specifically a spastic children's foundation. I lay down on the cot and fell asleep, unaware of the multitude of bad things that would soon happen.

That first night I woke up crying and would not stop. I wanted to go back to my grandmother. After Ruby complained that I was keeping her up, I was led out through her room, across the plush carpet, past her cluttered vanity table and her desk, and around the twin bed, covered with a floral quilt, in which she'd been trying to sleep.

Jill and my father sat me down in the living room. It was far into the night and Jill was tired and fed up. Even as a newlywed in a sheer pink nightgown, she looked sallow, craggy and thin. She was a tiny woman with closely cropped black hair and small sagging breasts. The shrivelled brown of her nipples showed through the nightgown and I was embarrassed. I had only met her two or three times before. I have no recollection of those meetings. I do remember that my father told me that Jill was the adopted daughter of a Chevrolet mogul and renowned philanthropist who belonged to the Standard Club. Supposedly he owned a dairy farm in Elkhorn, Wisconsin.

According to my grandmother, this was the second time that my father was marrying for money because my mother's family was also wealthy. Such marriages did not bode well, my grandmother said. By the time my father and mother separated, my mother had been disinherited by her parents and was living a dissolute life for which her parents blamed my father. I rarely saw or heard from her. When asked, my father said my mother drank too much, forged cheques and ran around with men. Even I remembered the time when I was three years old that her rich and disappointed father threw her, fully clothed and drunk, into a cold shower.

That night Jill told my father to slap my face if I didn't stop crying. A harsh little woman, I discovered then. She smoked cigarette after cigarette and hit me herself from time to time. I was not close to my father and I did not know how to express myself to him in words.

Early in the morning I was returned to my grandmother. My grandmother, a nurse, was used to my nervousness, and said, 'I'll give her a little phenobarbital to quiet her down' and she gave me a quarter of a grain. Then she fed me a bowl of delicious oatmeal. I have always remembered that bowl of oatmeal. I sat at the dining-room table while she stood sentry in the doorway of the kitchen. Tall and broad-shouldered, she had the same commanding blue eyes as my father, my brother and my eldest son.

The cuckoo clock sounded eight thrillingly familiar cuckoos and my grandmother was still in her housecoat. After breakfast, in a corner of the living room, I went to fix up my life behind the maroon leather armchair – some dolls, colouring books and crayons. Later in the afternoon my grandmother explained to me that she could not keep me now that my father was remarried and that in the evening I would have to go back to Jill's. But if I wanted, I could go and see if the Rosenblum children were home from school. If I were lucky, Alfred or Suzy, or both, would come outside to play handball with me for a while on a patch of cement in the back alleyway. Maybe Suzy would walk me over to Stony Island Park and swing me in the swings and my grandmother would give her thirty-five cents to buy an ice cream at Mitchell's if she kept me busy for an hour.

I went upstairs to the Rosenblums on the second floor. I hardly ever went to the third floor because the Wittenbergs didn't have kids my age.

The Rosenblums were fat and studious. Alfred was twelve and Suzy was eleven. They sweated profusely the few times we had ever played handball. It would be Suzy and me against Alfred. Or Alfred and me against Suzy. Their cheeks became puffy and red with heat. Alfred would slam the ball hard with the flat, sweaty palm of his hand. These games seemed to me intense and competitive but I never got hurt with Alfred or Suzy the way I got hurt if I played with my father or Teddy. Alfred and Suzy were my best friends, though, in retrospect, I did not know them well. That day Mrs Rosenblum, their mother, said that Alfred and Suzy were content to do their homework and that she didn't like them playing out in the alleyway after four-thirty because it was dangerous. Shortly after, I heard that they moved to their own house in Skokie, and I never saw them again.

At Jill's I was enrolled in the neighbourhood public school. I began to take piano lessons and ballet at the same school where Ruby took classes. For piano, a young teacher came to the apartment and sat next to me on the bench watching my fingers closely. I liked these lessons very much. Her name was Miss Linehan and she was pale and lightly freckled. She wore her long brown hair tied up in a bun. She lived in the neighbourhood but she wouldn't tell me exactly where, and I would try to trick her into revealing her address. We played this little teasing game for several weeks. I recall middle C and a song about rollicking sailors.

I understood nothing, as I do now that I am a mother myself, about notions of practice and steady improvement. I know now that parents size children up as far as ability and potential when they are putting out money for lessons. For example, I was given ballet slippers with elastic bands across the top of the foot but I wanted already to be dancing on pointe like Ruby, to have coloured tutus and tights draped over my empty twin bed. I wanted rolls of lamb's wool strewn over my light carpet. I wanted to be playing flats and sharps and chords and to be using both hands to play duets with Miss Linehan.

But I could not have put this yearning into words, and soon all my lessons were taken away because Jill said that I showed no talent.

Sometimes Blanche, a black maid, served us a formal dinner in the dining room. Dinner would be roast beef, potatoes and frozen peas or a piece of steak with a creamy noodle casserole on the side. Blanche wore a uniform, a powder blue dress to her mid-knee, and a white apron over her neck that tied around the waist with a bow at the back. Her hair was combed straight into a pageboy and she had thick blue plastic-framed glasses. She was light-skinned and petite. Her thin legs stuck out from the hem of her uniform like straight poles. Blanche wasn't pretty, but she was tidy and quiet.

Ruby was the same age as Teddy, thirteen, and she was physically mature, a fully developed woman, as my father would say. She had an olive complexion and dark eyes and short black hair cut like her mother's. It was expected that she and Teddy would be friends. Since my parents' divorce, Teddy had been living with my maternal grandparents and they were having a hard time managing him. When he was ten, he had been sent away to a military boarding school – and sent back. Some of the older students had placed a tape recording in his room saying they were going to cut off his dick for being a Jew. I didn't know him very well, when I think of how well my boys know one another. My father called him a troublemaker. But now I think, after raising two boys myself: what boy isn't?

At thirteen Teddy was a nervous boy, a leg bouncer when he was required to sit for more than a minute. He had turned into a greaser as soon as he started high school. He pomaded his hair and wore a black leather jacket. He loved Elvis Presley: he imitated Elvis's looks and mannerisms and had taught himself to play guitar. He could gyrate his hips and flutter his eyelids provocatively. He was interested in BB guns and motorcycles, and he carved a hole in the wall next to his bed with a pocketknife. Within the first few months Teddy was sent upstairs to live on the third floor with the Wittenbergs because he was fast becoming a juvenile delinquent, just as I was fast becoming an expert at listening through walls. He had tried to feel up Ruby's best friend, Amanda Epstein. He *had* felt up Amanda Epstein; he had touched her breasts. Besides the Wittenbergs could use the extra money that Jill paid for Teddy's room and board.

One time Teddy came downstairs to visit Ruby and me. I must have lured them onto the back porch with the promise that they could hold my hamster, Noreen. Her black beady eyes and twitching pink nose made her irresistible, even to teenagers. It was pleasant to pet her soft furry back.

Ruby showed me how a girl stuffs her bra. In fact the three of us gave ourselves huge tissue boobs. We used up a whole box of Kleenex. I stuffed the tissue under my undershirt, and Teddy packed it under his sweater. The three of us paraded for a while in a circle with our fake chests pressed forward, and, of course, Ruby's breasts looked enormous. After ten minutes or so, Teddy and I allied ourselves for the first and last time. We took the tissue from under our clothes where it had touched our cootied bodies. And we pushed our handfuls of tissue into Ruby's face.

Ruby backed away, told us to stop, threatened to tell. But we kept pushing and she kept backing away. Finally we pressed her so far up against the window that she slipped and fell backwards and hit her head on the radiator. For several seconds she was knocked right out. I don't know why we did it. Maybe Ruby said something about a recital or a trip to her Papa's dairy farm. Maybe she mentioned an outing to the Studebaker Theater to see Mary Martin starring as Peter Pan. Were Nana and Papa taking her to the Museum of Science and Industry and then out for Chinese on Wabash? Ruby often got treats that we didn't.

In the afternoon, a doctor, wearing a suit and tie and carrying a leather bag, came to the apartment. He went into Ruby's bedroom, and it was the first time that I ever heard the word concussion or of the area called Pill Hill, which was where a lot of doctors and lawyers lived in South Shore. Jill was told not to let Ruby sleep too much. And that if she was asleep, then she should be woken up every two to three hours. Ruby had a goose egg on the back of her head and a scrape. There had not been much blood. In the next two days, the door connecting our rooms was left open and I wandered more freely there than I had ever done before. And Ruby did not complain about me or Noreen making noise at night.

I was interested in talking to Blanche. I wanted to know about her. One day I went into the kitchen.

'How many children do you have, Blanche?' I asked.

'A handful.' I had heard she had two.

'Do you go to church on Sunday?' Once I had seen a Bible in her purse.

'Most time,' she answered, not looking up from the sink.

'Does the bus go very fast?' Sometimes she ran to 'catch it'.

'Unless it stuck between stations.'

'What are stockyards?' Jill had said that's where Blanche's husband worked.

'Chatterbox,' Blanche said. 'Blabbermouth. You ask too many questions.'

She shook her head disapprovingly and picked up her dust cloth. 'Shoo!' she said, waving the rag in my face. 'I got work to do. I'm not paid to be your babysitter.'

My father had always promised me a dog when things settled down. Not long after Ruby's concussion, he bought Lady from a pet shop. She was a mix of cocker spaniel and miniature poodle, a cute, tiny, black dog, a puppy, about eight weeks old. She was adorable, but as a family, we weren't equipped to care for her. My father was never around. Ruby was busy with her lessons, Teddy was upstairs and Jill was always asleep. No one seemed to have the slightest idea what to do with Lady, even me, though I had wanted her badly. After a few mistakes, she was relegated to the kitchen with Blanche. Blanche put newspaper out all over the kitchen floor and called it 'paper training'.

'There's nothing I can do to get out those stains on the carpet,' Blanche said to Jill. 'I don't want to use bleach, Miss.'

Blanche was angry that her kitchen was being used as a kennel. 'A devil of iniquity,' she grumbled when Lady 'missed' the paper and soiled the kitchen floor.

With not a word Blanche stopped coming to work.

The week Blanche quit Jill stayed in bed, sleeping most of the time. Once in a while she sat up when Ruby brought her a tray with a cup of black coffee and two slices of white toast. All day she did nothing as far as I was concerned. I don't think she read magazines.

Very soon my father got rid of Lady. I don't know where she went. My father got drunk and cried a lot; he liked dogs too.

Then Blanche came back to work, quieter than before. She would not start up any conversation with me. I tried. She did not even want to talk about the Bible.

Since my brother had moved to the third floor, I was in the spare room across from the kitchen. I was being punished for climbing onto the roof of the apartment building by way of the fire escape. I had to go to bed at seven o'clock without my supper for a week. Jill said I scared her when she didn't know my whereabouts.

Blanche let me keep the door open a crack. She would not let me come out of the room because that was my punishment for doing something dangerous and foolish. On the third day, I told her I was hungry, so she brought me a bowl of cereal. Tiny brown bugs were swimming in the milk. You had to have good eyes and a questioning mind to notice the bugs.

I held on to Ribbons, a stuffed black dog with a worn red ribbon collar. His girlfriend, Lady, a white stuffed dog, rested her head on my pillow. The sound of Noreen going round and round hypnotized me to sleep.

In those days once someone peeked in, I can't remember who. 'Are you still crying for that little dog? Don't you have anything better to do?'

I was in Jill's apartment being punished all the time. Eating bugs. Where was my father? Jill's father had fired him almost at once. Why was he never home if he wasn't selling Chevrolets? He still left every morning as if he were going to sell some cars. Then it came out. One time I was up, having just gotten off my last punishment, when my father came rolling in at ten o'clock. His face was glowing from the drink.

He said he had discovered private ponds and lakes off the Illinois highways. He was paying for fish by the pound – trout, perch, bass and mackerel, cleaned, flash frozen, ready to eat. 'It's peaceful work,' he said a little bashfully. 'Relaxing. I can drink and fish. Fish and drink. There's not a thing I'd rather do. Not a soul to bother me. A little rye makes the time go faster.

'You can catch a hundred pounds of catfish in half a day. Catfish weighing up to sixty pounds. Like monsters. Caught on bluegill heads.' But my father wasn't interested in catfish. They were scavengers, he said.

One Saturday when no one was around my stomach hurt and I lay down on Ruby's bed and vomited in my sleep. I stayed that way for several hours, wrapped like a mummy in my own filth, until Jill discovered me around four o'clock in the afternoon. Impassively Blanche stood me up in the bathtub and capably sponged me off. She let out the dirty water and washed out the tub, with me standing in front of her, naked and shivering. Then she filled the tub again with warm clean water and had me sit down. She let me soak for a long time and play with the scum of Ivory soap flakes that formed on top of the water.

But Blanche wants nothing to do with me, I said to myself. She looks down on me. She opens up the freezer and laughs under her breath when she sees all the cardboard packets of frozen fish. She thinks, What kind of father would send his own son to live upstairs with another sad Jew? She wonders what kind of a moron would lie for hours in her own puke.

I agreed with her completely. I wasn't going to argue. I knew she was superior.

I was starting to form opinions though. What does a girl think of when she is so alone? She comes to the opinion that her brother was causing the trouble between her father and her new mother. She blames him for everything, all the trouble, and wishes he were dead or eliminated even farther away than the Wittenbergs. As far away as the Rosenblums. She longs for Lady, the real dog, and Alfred and Suzy, her old and only friends, who have never called or written to her. She thinks Ruby looks sophisticated and physically developed and wishes that she had a Nana and Papa who took her shopping and dressed her in expensive clothes with all the accessories that go into making up a whole outfit. She thinks that Ruby has talent. She did tap and toe; she was playing duets with Miss Linehan on the piano. When the girl cried now, no one slapped her face. She did not cry. The door to the spare room was closed.

Little by little I was beginning to figure things out. Although I hated Teddy, he was an important source of information, and he increased my vocabulary. He was the one who told me what the f-word really meant. He said that the reason our father had custody of us was that he didn't want to pay alimony to our mother or her parents. He told me that Jill had a daughter the same age as me. That was her black-and-white portrait photograph in the gilded frame above Jill's dresser. She was a spastic child who lived in a special home and went to a special school for spastic children. Papa paid for it. Teddy said that Jill was addicted to Seconals.

He told me that Cynthia, the Wittenbergs' daughter, had fallen in love with a gentile boy. He told me what gentile meant. He said that Cynthia was planning to be married by a rabbi and a priest.

'In the rabbi's study?' I asked.

'No,' Teddy said. 'The rabbi's study is where you marry if you don't have enough family or friends to fill up the chapel or the congregational hall.'

Because he was a Holocaust survivor with a tattooed number on his forearm, Joe Wittenberg had gone sullen and morose about his daughter's intermarriage, according to Teddy. Every morning Mr Wittenberg and Cynthia passed me on the backstairs as I was on my way to school. Teddy told me that Mr Wittenberg dropped Cynthia at her office on his way downtown to a skyscraper where he worked on the twenty-second floor. Mr Wittenberg was always glum and frowning, but Cynthia looked happy. She was marrying for love. She wore pumps, pink lipstick, flounced skirts. She was a secretary. She had defied her father but he drove her to and from work. He wanted to know where she was and what she was doing.

One time I had a clear view of Jill and Ruby in the small bathroom in Jill's bedroom. I wasn't even hiding. Ruby was sitting on the closed toilet seat, crying. Jill stood next to her, examining her craggy face in the mirror over the sink. 'Why weren't you at my performance?' Ruby wanted to know. 'Where were you? All the other mothers were there. Were you sleeping?'

Then Ruby's eyes rolled upward in her head and her body went rigid. Foamy spittle gathered at the corners of her mouth and she threw her head back as if she were going to laugh. Instead she slumped over and fell to the floor. Her arms and legs were jerking like a fish flaps out of water. I had never seen her throw a tantrum. She was a cool and independent girl. Jill closed the bathroom door and started to scream. Again the pediatrician was called in from Pill Hill and this was the first time I heard the word epilepsy. The doctor gave Ruby some medicine and said that she would sleep for a long time.

On that same day my father went fishing. He called Jill on his way back from Pot o' Gold Pond near Lake Geneva to say that he would be late. He was slurring his words, she warned, the telltale sign that he'd been drinking. She held a nail file in her own hand and gave me a pair of manicuring scissors to protect myself against him when he came home. Then, she invited me into her bed and propped up by pillows, we sat next to each other waiting for my father. We waited for a fine and revelatory two hours in which I realized that great was my love for Jill.

Jill never broke the silence. I was going to point to the portrait photograph and ask some questions about her spastic daughter with the pixie haircut and the gap between her front teeth. But I had started to cherish the quiet between us. And I thought why risk it. The manicuring scissors meant a lot to me. I held on to them tightly. I wanted to keep them.

My father arrived with forty packets of frozen fish, his face reddened by drink and the sun. He took off his shirt and the contrast between his forearms and the skin above the elbows was like an equatorial line separating two hemispheres. Above the elbow his skin was white and hairless with an ugly heat rash of little pink pustules, and below the elbow, his arms were tanned and handsome. He held up his packets. 'The nutrition is locked in,' he said, running his words together. 'Right on the spot. The same way they do with peas and carrots. French fries. Poultry. This fish will have a long shelf life.'

We weren't interested. 'Don't come near us smelling of booze and fish,' said Jill. She pointed the nail file at him.

I said, 'Yeah, don't come near us.' I slowly moved my hand out from underneath the covers so that the manicuring scissors were in his line of vision.

Maudlin and confused, my father backed away.

Then I let go the manicuring scissors on top of the blanket and started to get up. 'I guess I'll go to bed now,' I said.

I followed my father into the kitchen. I was wearing Ruby's old yellow bunny pyjamas.

'That was a fine welcome,' said my father, quite sobered. He had begun to load up the refrigerator with his cardboard packets. 'I'm your father. It's over between us.'

'You're never here anyway,' I said, and went to the spare room. Our eyes had met. His were glassy and mine were full of disgust. The break had occurred and I didn't care. No one ate fish. No one hardly ate. When I thought of it later, I was surprised he didn't say anything to Jill. But by that time they hadn't a whole lot to talk about. Soon my father stopped coming home completely.

Several weeks later, in June of 1963, a few days after Pope John XXIII died, I found myself standing outside St. Philip Neri, the Catholic church on Merrill Avenue, around the corner from Jill's. Its great Gothic edifice was draped in mourning. I stood there for a while trying to understand vast sorrow. I knew that attached to the church was a convent where the nuns lived. I had seen them walking in their habits in the neighbourhood and I had heard them called penguins and I found this clever and amusing. I wished I could go and live in the convent because I knew the nuns who lived there didn't need to marry or worry about outfits. But I also realized they wouldn't accept me because of my religion. I had not yet learned the word conversion.

I didn't want to go back to Jill's apartment. Since the night of the manicuring scissors, her punishments had grown longer and more ruthless. Before they were married my father had hit me with a belt. But Jill was sentencing me to bed-at-seven-without-supper-and-stay-in your-room for a whole month at a time. She was also starting to talk about divorce. I could hardly wait. I was nine years old and I was sad and lonely. I heard Blanche's voice in my head. I had just learned the word iniquity. There and then I decided to become a writer.

I remember thinking these thoughts when Mr Freund, who lived in the first floor apartment across the courtyard, walked up with his blond cocker spaniel, Lucky. We stood and gazed at the church.

'The Pope was from peasant stock,' said Mr Freund solemnly. 'He was a man from humble origins.' Mr Freund tugged on Lucky's leash and made the dog sit down so that I could give him a pat. 'Nor is it Catholics alone who mourn his passing,' Mr Freund went on. 'Because the Pope loved mankind, all of mankind mourns the Pope. *Urbi et orbi*. In the city and in the world. The entire human family.' The people mourn for the Pope and I am a person, I thought. I am willing to mourn the Pope. Urby and Orby? Dog's names? This was before I studied Latin in the eighth grade.

Mr Freund said, 'A Pope leads a lonely life of work and contemplation. Never even shares a meal with another person.'

No one had confided so much to me in months. Already I was making up stories and wishes in my head. I wanted to explain how I was like the Pope. Alone and contemplative. Maybe I could get Mr Freund to adopt me. Or maybe he had a lady friend who would. My father had called Mr Freund a German Jew who had kept himself alive because he had come to America before the war. Therefore he had no tattoo on his forearm like Joe Wittenberg. No wonder he called his dog Lucky.

Mr Freund let me pat the dog as long as I wanted. In minutes, they were my best friends. The new Alfred and Suzy Rosenblum. No one, but no one, was as important to me as Mr Freund and Lucky.

'You like dogs,' said Mr Freund.

'Oh, yes,' I said. 'Very much.' I should go on walks with him and Lucky every day, I thought. I should organize my life so that I can join them in the afternoons. I should make this my number one priority.

'What happened to Lady?' Mr Freund asked. 'She was a cute little dog.'

I shook my head and said I didn't really know. This was already a lot of conversation for me because I was out of practice. I was afraid I wouldn't be able to keep up my end.

'Blanche came back,' said Mr Freund after a while. 'She doesn't like dogs.'

'Yep,' I said. 'Blanche came back.'

'Lucky seems to like you,' said Mr Freund. He looked away at the church façade. 'By nature, a cocker spaniel is a one-man dog.'

I nodded. I wanted to know more about canine behaviour. But Mr Freund had gone quiet. Then he turned and started to walk up the block. Of course I wanted to go with him. I was wild to follow. But I had learned how to take a hint. I got the feeling that Mr Freund and Lucky wanted to be alone to mourn the Pope. I wasn't really welcome to tag along in their grief.

I went home. Jill was sitting up in bed, wearing her pink nightgown, holding an ashtray. She looked sad, too. I wondered if she knew about the Pope. Get out of bed! I wanted to shout. I stood in her doorway. She was all I had. I wanted to tell her about my newly hatched plan to become a writer, an idea that had incubated a good fourteen minutes. I was thinking about moving to a bohemian district where I knew my mother was living in a cheap hotel. Once we had gone to a restaurant where the whole floor was covered in peanut shells.

'Mom,' I said softly. She turned her head to look at me. Her eyes were dull, a face of pallor and the lesson that money can't buy happiness. She took a puff on her cigarette.

'What are you staring at?' she said.

I shrugged my shoulders. I had nothing to say.

'Your father married me for my money,' she said. Then she let out a long thin trail of smoke. 'He didn't love me. I never should have married him.'

I nodded.

She said, 'Of course, you don't understand. You know nothing about life. Nothing at all. You couldn't.'

I was sick of her telling me what I knew and what I didn't. What I could do and what I couldn't. And I was sure that she had the wrong opinion about me. I had learned a lot, I thought, I understood life very well. I knew about failure and pity. About disappointment and boredom and neglect. I wasn't blind to the driving force of pain behind my father's eyes, Joe Wittenberg's tattoo, or Mr Freund's need to be alone with Lucky. I vowed to remember it all – Cynthia's flounced skirt, the carved hole in the spare room wall, Ruby's epileptic fit and the portrait of Jill's spastic daughter who was never referred to by name. I felt like a prophet with the power to transform childhood suffering into a pursuit of truth and justice. I promised myself I would commit to a discipline based on a system of hard work and rewards. I was ready to write a book. An autobiography. I'd read one by Helen Keller and found it inspirational. Even then I knew I would always love cuckoo clocks, leather armchairs, oatmeal and dogs.

Someone else had packed my patent leather purse for the wedding. It wasn't me. Did my grandmother not know even then that I was a girl who would never wear bows?

Jill and my father were separated for seven years before they finally divorced.

As for my hamster Noreen, she was buried in the back of Jill's apartment not long after the death of the Pope. She was supposed to live a thousand days and her number was up.

I went back to live with my grandmother, and Teddy went back to our mother's parents. We drifted apart.

One has to wonder how Alfred and Suzy Rosenblum decided to spend their lives.

There are modern opportunities for reunion. Yes, the world does spin. Spastics are now called persons with disabilities and there is Black History Month. What is today called an en suite was then called a bathroom in the bedroom. All that has passed is time.

Open, shut. Open, shut. Snap.

Home for Lunch

The eldest son, Ari, came home for lunch. After he ate, he entered the alcove of the bedroom where his mother, Celia Marx, was writing. He leaned over her shoulder and began to read out loud:

Dr Marcus, a Russian surgeon, took a leave of absence from the hospital, left his wife and children in Miami, and went to Africa on a mission of mercy. He was also in search of elephants, gorillas, and exotic birds of paradise. Instead he found there a continent driven down by famine and war. In the refugee camp, he became attached to a young boy he called the dancing bear. The boy was sick from contaminated water and grew thinner and thinner. Unable to save the child, the doctor began to fear for his own life and left before the start of the rainy season. The morning of his departure the starving people stormed a warehouse reputed to hold a supply of crackers.

'This is a terrible story,' said Ari. 'Africa is more than drought and disease. My geography teacher says the whole continent is under development.' His eyes were wide and blue and quite remarkable. She wondered what it would be like to see those eyes only on weekends, once a month, never again.

Celia shrugged. All morning long she had been thinking of leaving her family, but she was still in her bathrobe.

'Why is this Dr Marcus from the *former* Soviet Union?' asked Ari.

'I was thinking of the great Russian writers,' Celia answered with bitterness. 'How well they understood a soul in anguish.' Two months ago she had quit her job as a grade school teacher. She felt she was no longer able to take care of other people's children. It was hard enough to take care of her own. She herself had grown up without a mother.

'I take it anguish means conflict,' said Ari. 'Nowadays we call it point of view.' He read on.

Around the time Dr Marcus returned to Miami, Nurse Priscilla lost a baby who was born with multiple birth defects. Though she had prayed, consulted specialists, and tried to visualize a happy outcome, the child, whose head was misshapen – deformed by a little sac of fluid at the base of its skull – had died within the first week, on the seventh day, in fact, the same amount of time it took for God to create the world. Although there had been muffled talk and confusion about its vegetative state, there was no doubt the newborn felt pain. When Nurse Priscilla touched the little sac of fluid with the tip of her finger, the baby winced. The nurse lamented that during the brief flicker of his life, in which every effort had been made to resuscitate him, she herself, the child's mother, had not wanted to hold him.

As she watched him waste away, she was hounded by thoughts of the future. What if the baby dirtied himself when he grew up to be say, five, six, or seven and she slapped him and called him names? And what if he had trouble learning his ABC's, would she be sympathetic?

She was sick of it, already sick of the whole business of it, every night of the first and only week of the strain of bearing this child.

'She should've held him,' said Ari. 'He was her kid.'

'But she couldn't,' Celia replied sadly. 'She didn't know how.'

Ari's younger brother, Tom, was constantly getting into trouble. He broke and threw things. He couldn't sit still and found reading difficult. Mathematics was even more of a challenge. The measurement of angles almost impossible. Teachers and mothers were always calling about his disruptive behaviour. Much of the time at school he spent alone, isolated from the other children, and yet he stayed there over the lunch hour. He was in knitting club, still hoping for a friend. Often he woke up in the middle of the night. He barely slept. Up and down, always moving, he was frightened by the wind.

Ari bit his lip. Celia put her head in her hands. He continued to read.

On the day the baby died, Nurse Priscilla went through her closet and got a big plastic bag together for charity. She gave away all the skirts, slacks, sweaters, shoes and purses that she hadn't worn or used in the last three years.

Eight months earlier, her sister had given birth to a baby, a pretty, cherubic girl. The child was healthy and delightful from the moment she emerged. Three days under the bilirubin lights, that's all. The tinge of jaundice had cleared right up and it had been time to take the darling home. After her own baby died, Nurse Priscilla was consumed with jealousy every time she thought of her little niece.

A postcard arrived from her sister: *Don't come round. You frighten me.*

Nurse Priscilla began to question her own heart's capacity to love and whether the nervous system was indeed designed to experience ecstasy. I need more yellow in my life, she told herself. But most of the time, she felt like an actor impersonating a human being.

'I hate to tell you, Mom,' said Ari, 'but this is getting worse and worse.' He read:

Then Nurse Priscilla's boyfriend went off to Calgary. There he got involved in a pyramid scheme that promised to make him rich from the sales of an Australian tree oil extract called melaleuca. Supposedly the Aborigines had used it with great success in the treatment of rashes and infections.

Celia lifted her head and looked at her son. He was frowning. His father invested in risky business ventures, too. When she had first met him, he had liked to gamble, and she'd mistaken recklessness for ambition. Recently he'd been convinced of opportunity in Alberta. Sometimes he came home late at night. When Celia was very tired and the children were in bed. She put her head back down. Ari read:

By now Nurse Priscilla had started having coffee with Dr Marcus in the hospital cafeteria. Her pale, freckled cheek aroused his pity. And she had seen him take vials. Syringes were missing. Together they began to steal Fentanyl, a synthetic opiate, from the medicine supply cabinet.

One Tuesday morning, after surgery, as had become their habit, Dr Marcus and Nurse Priscilla snuck upstairs to a bathroom on the fifth floor of Geriatric. Dr Marcus filled a syringe while Nurse Priscilla wrapped a rubber tourniquet around her arm. He thumped up her vein. *'Way down yonder in the land of cotton,'* she sang in a tinny soprano as he injected her, and then after performing the same procedure on himself, he slumped back against the wall. A dense fog settled in around his body. The glare of a fluorescent bulb was scorching his eyes.

'This stuff'll kill you,' said Dr Marcus. 'Shark's teeth. Turn off the light.'

Then he watched as the nurse's hand crawled towards the switch shaped like a shell. 'It's ridiculous, I know it,' he heard himself mutter.

'There's no excuse,' said Ari. He shook his head in gloomy disappointment. But he read:

In the dark, Dr Marcus lay back against hard surfaces, let the inky blackness bleed into him. Gauzy bandages formed around his brain, as if he were wrapped in white muslin, a shroud-covered corpse. He wanted to call out, but it was as if his throat was filled with rocks. Those rocks now began evolving into soft, white, warm loaves of bread. He could tear those loaves apart and feed chunks to the dying boy in the refugee camp. As the warm bread rose up, expanding in his throat, Dr Marcus was afraid he was choking. He tried to cough and the loaves disappeared.

The cramps in his stomach were worsening. Waves of nausea lapped over him. Here I am in the centre of the jungle, he thought. And the roots of the trees are knotted. The flapping of wings sounds voodoo rhythms. I've got four kids at home waiting for breakfast.

Ari paused to steady his voice, and read:

A good part of the night had been spent in Emergency trying to repair the legs of an adolescent boy. Before the boy went under, he was begging, *begging.* 'Can you make me walk, doctor? Doctor, make me walk.' Overcome by grief and lassitude, Nurse Priscilla told the boy to pray for a miracle. For hours, Dr Marcus scraped metal and bone out of knee joints. But the boy's legs could not be saved.

Dr Marcus thought of his wife. If it was eight o'clock, she was already on her psychiatrist's couch covered up in the coat she used like a security blanket.

He was convinced she was the only girl who walked around Miami in the winter jacket she brought down from Toronto.

Dr Marcus lifted his head. He felt the need, quick and insistent, to be away from Nurse Priscilla, the hospital, everything that had gone wrong in the surgery.

'What were you thinking when you wrote this?' Ari said. His gaze was stern, a reprimand. 'It sounds as if someone else wrote it. Not you.'

Celia turned away. She would not meet his remarkable eyes. She imagined him finding her bathrobe on the kitchen floor. Daddy would be forced to explain. 'All that's left of Mommy,' he'd say. 'She gave us the best years of her life.' Maybe he could have the robe bronzed. Like baby shoes. So the boys wouldn't forget her. She sighed.

Ari asked, 'What happened to the boy's legs?'

'Drive-by shooting,' said Celia. 'A victim of gang violence.'

'How did the bullets hit?'

'Ricocheted, I guess.'

'I'd be careful about that one. Maybe you should consult a ballistics expert.'

'A ballistics expert!' Celia was sorry she had let him start.

He was watching her. 'You've got a lot of ideas, Mom,' he said. 'Quite an imagination. Carpet the "M".'

'Carpe diem,' said Celia. 'That's the problem.'

'Have you met these sorts of people?'

'No one you know.'

'C'mon, Mom, you know what I mean. You're being self-effulgent.'

'Indulgent. Self-indulgent.'

'What does "Geriatric" mean?' he asked.

'Old folks. The last stretch of life. The end of the line.'

'You should get out more. You're always so tired. Daddy's a good conversationalist. Go to a party. Sit next to him.'

Ah! she thought, Daddy was not a bad man, though his temper

was short. He was a child of Holocaust survivors, obsessed with the historical Jesus, unwilling to buy anything German. His parents' first child, a girl, had died during the war. He'd been brought up on tales of starvation. After a rage, he usually went grocery shopping. Celia always felt a little sorry for him.

Last summer they had tried to rekindle their relationship in noisy ways. They had gone to where a lot of people gathered – street fairs, open-air concerts, outdoor carnivals. He had talked about taking her down to Miami to show her where he had vacationed as a boy. But they had argued about everything. Once he knocked a potato out of her hand over a comment she made about being the only one in sixteen years of marriage to have ever cleaned the bathroom. His family called her the Salad Queen.

'It's phony to call her "Nurse Priscilla,"' said Ari. 'Are you listening? Just call her Priscilla. Plain and simple. Nobody calls their nurse "Nurse."'

'Okay,' said Celia. 'I guess you have a point.' Then she thought, I should be able to call her what I want. I have a few rights left, don't I?

'Are you thinking of seeing a shrink?'

'What makes you say that? Where'd you learn that word?'

He smiled. 'Why don't you put in a few farts? Nothing like a few farts to brighten things up.'

Celia saw him marvel at his wit. Then he wanted to know: 'What did my teacher say about my report card? I've got a feeling you're all worked up over nothing.'

'Probably. Maybe so.'

'One more question. How does it end?'

She could not answer. Ari pressed his hands on her shoulders.

'Anyway,' he said, 'this Nurse Priscilla is not like you at all. You would always love me no matter what. You are definitely not an actor in the role of a human being. You're my mother. Mom?'

Celia pushed back her chair and the wheels rotated across the wooden floor like a ship sailing away. She went to lie down on her bed. Curling up on her side, she began to cry. She had not cried in a very long time and never like this in front of her son.

Ari's expression turned grave. 'What's the matter, Mom?' He sat down beside her. 'You're not suicidal, are you, Mom? Don't you want to be my mother?'

Celia opened one eye. Ari would not have believed her thoughts. She could tell him that some mothers do decide against their children. Once in a while her mother sent her a greeting card signed "Love, Mother" from Phoenix or Cheyenne or from her last address in Skokie, Illinois, with a couple of bucks folded into the envelope. Don't spend it all in one place, thought Celia. She didn't need a therapist to figure out that many nights as a child she had gone to bed hungry.

He was looking at himself in the mirror above her dresser.

'I've got a pimple the size of Manhattan,' he said.

Celia stopped crying. The end of all her explorations would likely be to make another meal.

Ari asked, 'What's the title of this story going to be?'

'"Effigies from My World".'

'What's an effigy?'

Celia propped herself on her elbows. 'An effigy is a representation. Like a doll would stand in for a human being.' She considered it best not to mention hanging or public burnings.

'It's not your world, Mom. Believe me, it's another world completely. This world has nothing to do with you.'

So you think, she thought. In the pocket of her robe was a note from Tom. He had written *If you want to get ride of me, go rite ahed.* 'I wish you wouldn't fight with your brother,' she said. 'He's got enough problems.'

'As Hillel said, "Love your neighbour as yourself. The rest is comedy."'

'Commentary,' said Celia. '"The rest is commentary." That's what he said.'

'Oh, Mom, you're a genius.'

Celia sank back on the bed. His admiration hurt her. She thought of Tom. He used to have an endearing smile. But now he often looked unsure. When she asked for his cooperation, he sniggered and said, 'Bite me!' Or, 'Eat my shorts!' Celia had the urge to travel to a warm place and walk by the sea. She longed for a sister.

Now Ari went to get ready for school. Celia got up and returned to her desk. She wrote:

Big Norma was doing laundry all weekend for Dr Marcus's family in West Palm Beach to pay Mrs Marcus back for borrowed money. Big Norma's back ached, and she was sure of a whole day of bending down. Today was Sunday, and she was skipping church to make good on her loan. Her seventeen-year-old son, Cookie, a.k.a. Oodles, drove her to the bus stop. His posted bail needed repaying.

Now Big Norma looked at her son carefully in the bright light of morning. She did his dusting and folded his socks into a neat stack. Washed his underwear, too.

She opened the car door, lifted her large body outside into the heat, and closed the door behind her. Then she walked away, pressing her shoulders back and her head forward.

(At the hospital it had been hinted that Big Norma stole the Fentanyl to support her son's street habit. When she heard the rumour, Big Norma eased up on her scrub brush and uncoiled like a cobra into her proud, erect posture. 'The good Lord taught me forgiveness,' she said. 'I got my own sorrows and prayers to float down the river. Truth will prevail.')

Then Ari came up behind Celia. 'Look here,' he said, softly touching her neck. 'My science teacher says this vein shows how smart you are. Intelligence comes from how much blood is pumped to the brain.'

'That's idiotic,' said Celia. She turned around to face him. 'I don't know what they're teaching you.'

'Aw, Mom! You worry too much about my education. No need, no need.' He patted her head like a dog. 'This afternoon, in history, we're studying sarcophagi.'

'How interesting,' she said, and brushed his hand away.

'When you die, I hope you'll leave everything to me.'

'What do you mean "when I die?"' Celia's head was sore from crying. 'Why bring that up?'

But he was gone. The front door slammed behind him. Celia looked around the room. It was all too familiar. The marriage bed, the bookshelves, the family photographs tucked into the mirror. She hadn't realized how long all this growing up would take. An empty suitcase waited under the bed. But Ari would always want to do the leaving. She wrote:

Time passed, but soon enough, on a Monday morning, Big Norma was coming into the bathroom on the fifth floor of Geriatric to replace a toilet paper roll, with a pail of sudsy water slapping against her knee. She pushed her broad backside against the unlocked door, and Dr Marcus and Nurse Priscilla were caught in a trapezoid of watermelon light.

'My goodness, John the Revelator!' Big Norma exclaimed. 'They thought me a robber, but lookie here, what the cat brought in. Now, ain't I a woman?'

Dr Marcus bought himself a puppy and moved into a motel room not far from the ocean where he spent a lot of time getting himself back into shape by playing beach volleyball. At the rehab meetings he went to in a corner church two blocks away, he listened to men more miserable than he, young junkies and Vietnam vets. The evenings he spent alone recalled to him the literature of his youth, writings on work and death and suffering. Tolstoy's chronicles of Sevastopol, surgeries performed without anesthesia. Babel's bloody Cossack war. Chekhov's Sakhalin, an island of cold exile. The affable and ineffectual Uncle Vanya who steals a bottle of morphia.

He had not forgotten the number of wives kicked to death in the pages of Gorky.

In spite of his hardships, Dr Marcus realized that his was the life of good fortune; his motel allowed pets! His own parents had suffered persecutions under the Nazis and Stalin. His father to this day was haunted by the shoutings of Goebbels. His mother had used the German word *heimweh*, which meant a prisoner's longing for home.

Often Dr Marcus cried because he missed his kids.

It was almost four o'clock. Rain was coming down hard, the sky emptying of light. Any minute now her sons would be home, bounding up the stairs, a race of mendicant children demanding snacks. Celia sat staring at her words. Playing a game with them of omens and signs. She wrote:

Nurse Priscilla ended up in Cleveland where she went to work in an orphanage with babies born to mothers addicted to crack cocaine. She proved to be very good with the children whose attention spans were short. She was able to calm their frequent rages. Her work required a constancy of patience. In her spare time, she began to paint and sculpt using the lives of women writers as her inspiration. Her works bore such titles as *Two Jugs of Milk Left at Cribside: A Tribute to Sylvia Plath: Never Again!* A simple mound of clay, rather untidy, with crushed dry leaves and broken bits of glass, was called *An Unmarked Grave: Jane Bowles in Malaga: You Are Not Forgotten.* And a painting of the palace at Fontainebleau she entitled *Katherine Mansfield: A Mystic's Call: I See Your Ghost.* Often incorporating text as one of her techniques, she scrawled across a monochromatic snow scene a lyric from the poet Marina Tsvetaeva: *Yes, I suppose I grabbed at Spring.*

In a yoga class offered at the neighbourhood community centre, she learned to meditate, closing her eyes and intently holding the imperfect face of her lost child for long periods of time in her mind's eye. Finally, she was able to drop a postcard to her sister: *I'm a little better now. If you want, call me. Love, Cilla.*

Her old boyfriend wrote: *Melaleuca über alles.* He had made twenty thousand dollars in four months.

Nurse Priscilla bought herself some new clothes.

When she heard that Dr Marcus had been reinstated at the hospital on a part-time basis, Nurse Priscilla telephoned him. He told her he had run into their former patient, the young amputee, on the Orthopedics ward, hobbling down the corridor on his new prosthetic limbs. 'You would think a boy like that could end up in trouble. You expect to get a call from the police in the middle of the night about a boy like that. But he said he'd be dancing,' Dr Marcus reported to Nurse Priscilla. 'He said he'd be doing a jig in no time at all.'

Celia paused. She wanted to see Tom happy. She wanted to see him laugh. She wanted to be able to comfort him. She wrote:

Dusk was passing into night. It had already rained. The smell of the swamp was not far off. Big Norma walked along the highway, fanning herself with palmetto, beating at the air. She passed a small graveyard off to the side of the road and thought of her mother, up in Illinois, buried in such a place as this with a little white cross for a marker.

She wrote:

There is no heaven on earth. Hope must be devised. Pretend.

Celia got up from her desk. Ari would seek her out for a promise of the future. She would be making dinner. He would bump alongside her. He would want to know. 'Are you better now, Ma? Are you better?' He would want to see courage. He would want to see optimism. Of course she would want to tell him the truth. Even if that meant telling a lie. She must make a point of kissing Daddy hello. Then with good conscience Ari can go fight with his brother.

Five Months

Pa is dead and there's no bringing him back. This is a fact of life. I've got to face it. A shadow was stretched across the ceiling. I could make out an arm, a hand, a pointed index finger. What threshold is Pa crossing? I wondered. For a while I stared at the ceiling and watched the shadow dissipate into light. I turned over in bed and closed my eyes. Later in the morning I tossed the booklet *How to Explain Death to Children* into the recycling bin. My kids didn't need it. They'd been privy to the whole process. Harry shouted and threw tantrums for three weeks after the funeral.

Davey said, 'It was easier to say goodbye once I saw the body in the coffin. I knew he wasn't there.'

'Where do you think Pa is?' I asked. 'Do you think he's on the other side?'

'He's not here,' said Sheldon, my husband, Pa's son. 'He's not calling. I haven't heard from him. Have you?'

In his coffin, Pa looked cleaned-up and shaven, waxen and smooth, shroud-covered, completely changed in a day, with a little plastic baggie tucked in next to him that Davey saw first. In the baggie was some sand, twist-tied and labelled Dirt from Israel. Five months from beginning to end. Look how fast a person disappears.

It was early January and Pa had been waiting inside while the snow piled up around his house on Hove Street. Frail and aggrieved, he answered the door. At the kitchen table I apologized; Sheldon bent his head. How could we make a ride back to Toronto in a station wagon sound so difficult when Pa had crossed Siberia on foot?

'I was thinking I'd lost a family,' Pa said, consumed by old fears. He'd phoned the hotel, the border crossing, the highway police. He didn't want to hear any excuses about weather. Or car trouble in West Virginia. (No, Pa, the Klan didn't overrun us.) He wasn't interested in how we'd spent our time in Florida. There could be no explanation for why we hadn't called him. 'In America everyone is crazy. Do you know how these Americans carry guns? Use guns. Especially the blackies.'

Most of the time I didn't mind Pa's opinions. He said stupid things. Made silly comments. Far-fetched, even ignorant. Long ago I'd warned the children. Let your grandfather's words fly over your head.

I could tell Pa was sick. He was yellow and shrunken, his belt pulled three notches tighter than it had been two weeks before. He held his head in his hands. He said he hadn't eaten in days. He was constipated, too. 'Buy red grapes, buy green grapes, seeds and seedless. Buy grapefruit!' he said. 'I've got a taste for apples. Bring me the bill and I'll pay you back.' I knew better than to argue. Pa was frugal. He never took lightly the subject of debt. In every kitchen cranny were paper scraps, handwritten in black ink, legends of money spent and owed.

At the grocery store, Harry said, 'Is Pa going to be okay? Is he going to keep smoking? Who'll get his car?'

I made Pa chicken noodle soup from the can. I cut all the fruit I bought into itty-bitty pieces.

In the afternoon Pa vomited and I had to leave the laundry and rush back over to his house. I helped him change out of his robe and into a fresh one. I tried to scrub the carpet. I called his doctor.

In Emergency a nurse stripped off his clothes and set up the IV. Pa burped, groaned, peed himself. 'See what becomes of a man,' he said. Never before had I noticed the deplorable state of Pa's T-shirts and underwear, his worn leather watchband, fastened by a grubby and fraying piece of string.

Four nights in Emergency waiting for a room and a diagnosis – fecal impaction, gallstones, appendicitis, pneumonia. What was it? Why not start treatment right away? I visited Pa in the middle of icy nights, gave him orange juice through a straw, listened to his stories with a new intensity. He had done what he could for his wife, he said, more than his best, in the way of doctors and clinics and private nursing care. He hadn't money but no expense was spared. His efforts had added three years to her life. Three extra years! It was nothing to sniffle at. I agreed Pa was a hero.

And Europe. How glorious was Europe in his childhood! There wasn't divorce, lunacy or retardation. It had been a near perfect world. I couldn't imagine.

Pa's last girlfriend, Svetlana, wasn't mentioned. He'd found her in a Russian food shop, buying sprats. She was a mathematics professor from the Ukraine.

'Do you know how old she is?' Pa's voice had boomed proudly. 'Thirty-seven.'

Around his house she walked, doe-eyed and barefoot, making intelligent conversation. 'You add eucalyptus to the pot of steam … Trotsky deserved to be killed … a schism between the Russian and Greek Orthodox churches … the first king of Moscow … I was thinking of the Tartars.'

Pa drank only instant coffee; Svetlana preferred fresh-roasted and ground. Quickly her son, Vladimir, learned the difference between Pepsi and Coke.

Pa said, 'Vlad's a kid. Eight years old. You can't leave him at home.' By and large Pa was inclusive.

Sheldon's brother, Michael, showed up at the hospital. Pa was happy to see him. Michael was certain I was making a big deal out of nothing. It was probably dehydration, he said. His granddaughter, Rebecca, had once been dehydrated. Dehydration was frightening.

Michael offered to give me a ride home. It was past seven and cold outside. We walked to the parking garage without much to say. Then we were in Michael's car. It was a fancy new car with a talking screen on the dashboard. I decided to comment.

'What kind of car is this?' I asked. I'd heard Davey say that the car cost eighty thousand dollars.

'It's just a car,' Michael said. 'I don't get excited about these things like I used to. If you want the seat to heat up, I'll press the button.' I nodded. Soon my buttocks were warm. 'It's working,' I said.

Michael made several calls on his cell phone as he drove. He'd been away in the Dominican Republic. His vacation was beautiful.

Much nicer than Florida in his opinion. The hotel was grand. 'Quite a surprise,' he said of his father's illness. 'He shovelled the first snowfall. Was always strong as a bull. Never had a headache a day in his life.' Then he called Barbara, his wife. 'Where do you want to eat? Wherever you like. The problem is we don't have any dislikes. Heh, heh.'

Michael pulled into our driveway. I invited him in and he declined. He said, 'Pa's eighty-four. Sooner or later we all have to die. We'll sell his house as it is.'

Sell! Who said sell? The house was large for an old man living on his own, but Pa never wanted to sell. He loved his house, a split-level, built in the fifties. He never stayed away from it for long.

At home Sheldon was making dinner. The kids were watching 'Who Wants to Be a Millionaire?' I took off my coat and went into the kitchen. I wasn't hungry.

'"We all have our own lives." That's what Michael said, heh, heh,' I reported to Sheldon. 'He would never stick his hands in Pa's fruit salad vomit.' Then I said, 'Pa is my life.'

'Why?' asked Sheldon. 'He's my father.'

'I feel like a real daughter,' I said, glaring. Sheldon didn't change. He would never understand what it was like growing up without a father, the lifelong and barely subconscious stratagems devised to escape the fate of being fatherless. Even in fairy tales we fatherless girls were a marginalized group. Locked up in towers, frozen in coffins, eaten by wolves. Often murdered. Sheldon was cutting up mushrooms. He said, 'Barbara thinks Pa shouldn't have had any green fruit. She brought over twenty prunes before they went away. She said Pa didn't need any of the green stuff. Fresh fruit was the wrong thing to feed him.'

'Twenty prunes,' I said. 'The last of the big spenders. *Darkness was cheap and Scrooge loved it.*' I washed my hands. I said, 'I should know better. When are the rich ever magnanimous? I feel sorry for Michael. How he surrounds himself with things. He must feel impoverished in other areas of his life.' Then I said, 'Pa was dying for grapes. He wanted fruit. He was starving.' I started to cut up red peppers. 'Pa probably doesn't love me. Do you think he loves me?'

'Probably not,' Sheldon said. 'He's probably not capable. You'll have to settle for the kindness of one human being to another.'

I was dicing onions. I had tears in my eyes. 'Michael and Barbara are blaming Pa's sickness on fruit salad. That's absurd. Totally absurd.'

'Maybe you should've left out the kiwi,' said Sheldon.

On Day Five Pa was moved to the seventh floor. He had gotten better in hospital. Hope was rekindled and alive. Sometimes he sat up in bed all day chatting. He passed the earphones around when Liz Taylor was on *Larry King Live*. 'I've always loved her,' he said. I was proud. I felt I had saved his life.

To keep everything in perspective I learned that the Schecter boy, who lived in the neighbourhood, was on the same ward as Pa, and in a coma just three rooms away, and he was less than twenty-one years of age. No one could believe what had happened to Arnie Schecter, not even Pa. The nurses dressed up like astronauts before they went into his room.

On Day Eight, the day of the diagnosis, which was lung cancer with a second primary in the kidney, Pa ate a nice breakfast. He seemed rejuvenated. In the morning the oncologist took Sheldon and me into the doctor's lounge. The doctor was a young man, dark-eyed and laconic. I thought he looked like a guy who could ride around all day on camels. He never met my eyes with his cool black ones, I figured because I wasn't blood.

I wanted to tell him that blood didn't matter in times like these. What was blood compared to affection?

That afternoon Michael and Sheldon were at the hospital.

'Here's what Michael said,' Sheldon informed me. '"I'd like you to make a stipulation for each of my children. And for Melissa's daughter, Rebecca, your one great-grandchild." That's what Michael said.'

I thought of Michael's four children – Melissa, Howard, Rory and Holly, whose lives were filled with bounty and privilege. And I thought of Melissa's daughter, Rebecca, a fair-haired sprite with pale blue eyes. Why did any of them need Pa's money?

But it wasn't my business. When it came to money, affection wasn't as thick as blood.

Sheldon had called me at home. 'Michael suggested that Pa leave each child a monetary sum,' he said, 'say three or five thousand dollars. So that they'll remember him. Barbara's mother is bequeathing the kids five thousand dollars each so that they'll remember her. Michael asked Pa, "Don't you want to be remembered?"'

I had been making a shopping list. I put down my pencil. 'I'll remember Pa,' I said. 'Davey and Harry will remember Pa. They don't need his money to remember him. Pa is his own bequest.'

Pa's hospital room overlooked the city. He had a beautiful view. He was sitting up in his bed by the window. 'A north wind is blowing,' he said. 'And a north wind is the coldest.' Chimney smoke gave him a sense of direction. Experience gave him knowledge. His observations of the natural world endeared him to me.

On Thursday evening I went straight to the hospital. I liked my time alone with Pa. 'An angel gave me a bath today,' he said. 'A nurse like an angel. She washed me all over and gave me a shampoo.' His hair was soft and white like feathers rising up from his bald head.

He'd been telling stories about his youth. I hung on his words. 'How about your grandfather?' I said. 'What do you remember?'

'I used to sit in his lap and play with his long black beard. When he retired from the law, Prince Radziwill had a stone house built for him. He gave him twenty-eight acres of land. And if my grandfather had an extra farthing, he bought me a chocolate.'

'Tell me about your grandmother.'

'My bubbie had eleven children and five of them went to the United States. When she died we found a huge bed sock.' Pa made a motion from his waist to his foot. 'A sock full of money and that's how they paid off my father's share of the flour mill. We were never rich but we had enough.'

Pa turned over on one side. He was in a ruminative mood. 'Rory would spend the money in a pub,' he said. 'Jews don't go to pubs. The worst people go to pubs.' Rory was twenty-two, Michael's youngest son. I liked Rory. He had a child's face. He'd never lost his baby fat.

'Rory's not a big drinker,' I said. 'I don't think you have to worry.'

'When I gambled at his age, we played for five cents. Ten cents at the most. It was a lot of money. Once against Uncle Motti I had four kings. I bet two-fifty and he had four Johnnies. He bet five dollars and I said I'd stick. I was afraid to lose. But when I laid down my cards, he was mad like hell.'

I laughed. How funny Pa was. Then Sheldon came with the boys. Davey kissed Pa and sat on the end of his bed.

Harry liked Mr Guryadev who was in the bed next to Pa in 27-A. Mr Guryadev looked like a middleweight prizefighter, but he'd lost the capacity to talk. His son was a pharmacist. Harry took Mr Guryadev's pee bottle from his crabbed hand. He emptied it in the toilet. Then he helped Mr Guryadev take a sip of ice-chip water.

'What does Harry have with Mr Guryadev?' Pa wanted to know. He liked his attention undivided. 'Why does he need to go tearing off to help him? Let Guryadev yell and the nurses'll come.'

Harry's like me, I thought. His affection doesn't depend on blood.

Pa said Mr Guryadev had kept him awake. 'He was shouting in the middle of the night. "I'm going to kill you. Don't hurt me." In the night he talks plenty. I think he's a Litvak.' Pa stopped, and lowered his voice to a whisper. 'The son was here today. Both legs have gangrene. They mentioned amputation.'

Harry came over to Pa's side of the room. 'Mr Guryadev talks. I just heard him say "Go, go sleep."'

Pa grimaced at Harry's enthusiasm. 'He's not even a relative,' Pa said and shrugged. He had his own opinions. He was lying sidewise on the bed. His head was propped on his hand. He wanted to talk about luck and how his was better than his friends.

'Freedman lived to be eighty,' Pa said. 'Goldstein made it till eighty-nine. Slutsky died young, in his sixties. A massive heart attack. You couldn't save him.'

Sheldon nodded. He adjusted Pa's blankets.

Pa went on. 'My house is paid up. And there's enough for my funeral. I know how much I have. Down to the cent. If I decide to give each grandchild three thousand dollars ... or five thousand dollars, I will.'

Davey and Harry were quiet. They looked at Sheldon and me.

Then a cough, a splutter, a letting go of the bowel and bladder. I discovered Pa's dry pad had been taken out from under him and never replaced by the angel nurse. The bed was ruined. A shooing of Harry and Davey out of the room. Go wait in the lobby of the oncology ward. You'll see Arnie Schecter's name on the nurse's board and wonder about the mystery of life. Pull the curtain around Mr Guryadev. Quick.

I wiped up Pa, the floor, crumbs from the carrot cake I'd brought him for a snack, bits of squash and kernels of corn from lunch. Sheldon got Pa to the bathroom while I stripped the bed. I found the laundry hamper and then I took fresh green linens from the rolling shelf unit in the corridor.

Twenty minutes later Sheldon began to turn the handle at the foot of Pa's bed to lower him down. Then Michael and Barbara walked into the room.

'Hi, Pa,' Barbara said. 'Why don't we get you up to sit in the patients' lounge?'

'Let him stay in bed,' I said. 'We just got him cleaned up.'

'I brought you some food, Pa,' said Barbara. 'Meat and potatoes.'

'He's had enough to eat,' Sheldon said. 'You're not hungry, are you, Pa?'

'Pa, do you want to go to the lounge?' Barbara said. 'The exercise won't kill you.'

'C'mon, Pa,' Michael said, lifting the old man by his thin elbow. 'C'mon. Have a bite.' Pa didn't protest and they led him out of the room.

The next day, in the morning, Pa fell and hit his head when the nurse took him down for tests. He had a bloody cut above his left eyebrow. He remained upbeat. His room was filled with family visitors. It was late Friday afternoon.

'The test was fast,' Pa said. 'Why? Machines are making it. And machines are fast and they talk. When it pinches the kidney, a man's voice cries out, "I got 'em. Pom!"'

'How do you feel, Pa?' I said. 'That cut looks nasty. Does your head hurt?'

'The way I feel now, I can live another year. We can make dinners. I'll make a chicken soup. I'll make a brisket if I feel like this. I got 'em. Pom!'

'Why don't we get you to come out tomorrow night to celebrate Michael's birthday?' said Barbara. 'We'll get you a day pass.'

Sheldon looked up from the magazine he was reading. 'A day pass?' he said. 'We just got him into the hospital. Forget about it.'

She's hardhearted, I thought, a cold woman, a stone. I tried to keep my voice neutral. 'It's freezing outside,' I said. 'He's frail. He could slip.'

'I don't want to go, Mikey,' Pa said. 'The doctor said I may have bloody pee. Or cramps from the test. I don't want to take a chance.'

'It's Michael's fifty-fifth,' Barbara said sternly. 'You won't want to miss it.'

What's the big deal? I thought. Michael's not a kid. The guy's fifty-five.

'I was over at your house today,' Michael said, moving on. 'To check on the heat and pick up the mail. I had a look around.'

'Go ahead,' Pa said. He lay back on his pillows. 'Be my guest.'

'There are things in the house in which I'm interested,' said Michael.

He sounded as if he had intense feelings about those things. It's just stuff, I thought.

Pa looked at me. 'You and Barbara will come over to the house and divide the crystal and china. And the silver. Take amicably what you want. You're not jealous people.'

'There's plenty of time for that,' Sheldon said.

'Pom!' said Pa. 'Don't worry.'

'I've got all your money,' Michael said. 'I've been investing it and paying you interest. You don't need the money any more. I'll give you a thousand dollars a month.'

Michael is comfortable with this line of conversation, I thought. He's like Pa.

'Right now I just want to feel better,' Pa said. He felt the cut on his forehead with the tips of his fingers. 'I feel okay.'

Michael pulled a large manila envelope out of his briefcase. He said, 'Here are your mortgages. I'll need your signature.'

Rory helped Pa to sit up. Michael put a pen in Pa's trembling hand. There were a lot of papers for Pa to sign. Sheldon shook his head and got up. He folded his magazine and went out of the room.

Pa said, 'Where do I sign?'

Someone on the ward cried out, 'Nurse! Code blue in 323.' Mr Guryadev groaned.

'Maybe there's a chance they can still remove the kidney,' Pa said when he'd finished signing all the papers. He sank down on the bed. 'That doctor who gave me the test can kiss mine ass. Tell him I want more salt on the smoked turkey.'

Rory shook his head at Pa's disintegration. 'Why don't we change the subject?' he said.

Hockey was the sport Pa was interested in. 'Gordie Howe was great,' said Harry. 'But Bobby Orr was the best.'

'Tim Horton had a hard shot,' Pa said.

'A great shot,' said Rory.

'Who do you think was the best Leaf ever?' Harry shouted.

'Davey Keon,' said Pa. He smiled. He loved the Leafs. He watched them every Saturday night. 'He was a smart player. He wasn't big. But he had heart. He was fast.'

Harry jumped up and clapped. Davey told him to settle down. 'Who watches *Hockey Night in Canada*?' Harry cried with joy. 'We do! Pa and me!'

That night Sheldon and I were talking in bed. 'There are more important things to think about than Pa's money or the stuff in his house,' I said. 'For example, Canada's food supply. Have we imported tainted blood meal that's being used as fertilizer on our vegetables?'

'Michael says that all Pa ever talked about was money.'

'It's no excuse,' I said, and asked, 'How did Michael become so callous? Why is he so unfeeling?'

Sheldon said, 'Maybe Pa beat him. Pa probably beat him.' He paused for a moment. 'Pa beat me, too. I'm also unfeeling.' Then he said, 'Don't idealize Pa, Alice.'

'I gave up on perfection long ago,' I said, trying to be funny. 'Lucky for you.'

Then I tried to make out Sheldon's face in the dark. I wanted to see his eyes. 'How about that forty thousand dollars Michael still owes you?' Sheldon had worked for Michael in the eighties. In the nineties Michael cut Sheldon's wages. It was just like Cain and Abel.

Sheldon took a deep breath. 'Yesterday Michael and I had lunch at the hospital. He still blames the recession. And I told him it was water under the bridge. I don't care any more.' He paused. 'I was that far from taking him to the Ministry of Labour. But for Pa's sake, I held back.' I saw him looking at me. 'Michael knows you don't like him.'

'Did I say I didn't like him?'

'It's pretty obvious you don't want to go tomorrow.'

'I'm confused, that's all,' I said. 'Families confuse me. I never really had one.' I turned over. 'Did I ever tell you how my father showed up drunk with a strange woman at my eleventh birthday party?'

'About a hundred times.'

'Anyway, there are more important things than Michael's birthday party.'

'Like what?'

'Like Arnie Schecter. I saw his mother at the hospital. A sensitive MRI shows no brain activity. But when he turned his head to the left, she said, she felt hope.'

Then we couldn't talk any more. We fell into a fitful sleep, back to back. At one point Sheldon woke up and nudged me. 'Do you think Pa will make it home from the hospital?' he whispered.

'Pom,' I said because I could think of nothing else to say. I lay awake for a long while.

In the morning Sheldon looked at himself in the bedroom

mirror. He said, 'Do I look like Michael? Do I have bags under my eyes? Michael has terrible bags under his eyes. At least I have my hair.'

I pitied Pa at Michael's birthday dinner. I felt sorry for the deterioration that couldn't be hidden. Pa stumbled in and created peril by the coffee table where the hors d'oeuvres were set out. Then Barbara yelled in from the kitchen. 'Don't knock anything over!' She hated commotion.

Pa no longer wore button-up shirts and belt-cinched pants. He was a skinny green monster, bug-eyed and jaundiced who swam in a sweat suit. His dentures, now grey, floated in his mouth.

One on each side, Davey and Harry helped Pa to the dining-room table. Everyone sat down while Barbara surveyed the passage of food trays down the long table. I looked around at Barbara's family. Her family couldn't be easy, I thought. Often you were stuck with blood.

Ira, Barbara's brother-in-law, piled heaps of food onto his plate. He was a large man with hair like a Brillo pad. 'I'm glad for every extra pound I have,' he said, looking at Pa. He puckered his lips as if he'd tasted something sour.

Meanwhile the act of sitting up was taking all Pa's energy. He was teetering.

Then he began to burp. At first his burps were short and quick like hiccups. 'If I hadn't gone to my doctor,' he said, almost choking, 'I wouldn't be in trouble.'

'What do you mean, Eppie?' said Barbara's mother, Claire. Claire was also in her eighties. But she was the kind of person about whom it was said, 'Oh, what a marvel', 'Still going strong', 'Sharp as a tack', 'She doesn't let herself go'. Claire played bridge. She golfed. She went to the symphony. She wore scarves and pendants. She was well coiffed and sturdy. It was almost cruel to see her in the same room as Pa. 'What do you mean you "wouldn't be in trouble"?' said Claire.

Pa couldn't answer. His sparrow's head was quivering. Rebecca stared at her great-grandfather as he swung his head in circles. Somewhere along his windpipe, air was trapped, constricting his breath completely. Arduously he kept whacking at the back of his neck with the flat of his hand until finally the burp was expelled with a loud 'Alleyoop'.

I knew what Pa meant. His doctor didn't care about old people. He'd ignored the low hemoglobin and the steady weight loss until it was too late. He hadn't admitted that blood in the urine was a very bad omen.

The salad had stopped in front of Barbara's sister, Elaine. Every so often I wondered what kind of relationship Barbara had with Elaine. Were they friends beyond the fact of being sisters? Or were they consumed by jealousies and comparisons? Would they offer each other their kidneys or bone marrow? I couldn't tell. There was no demonstrative affection.

'I'd like to go on a big adventure,' Elaine said. 'Some place wild.'

Wild adventure, I thought. Elaine and Ira on safari. Sometimes I wished I could just show up and have a few drinks for the sake of the family. And then head home.

'Cuba's a possibility,' Elaine mused. 'Though I hear everything's run down.'

'Pa went to Cuba,' Sheldon said protectively. He was cutting up Pa's chicken into very small pieces.

'Beautiful place,' Pa said, sputtering. 'Friendly people. Warm sun.'

'Michael is going fishing in Venezuela,' said Barbara. She took a sip of wine. 'Then we're off to Acapulco. To our time-share.'

All this talk of travel, I thought, when Pa has booked a one-way ticket to the grave. No one seemed to notice that he was about to topple off his chair.

Twenty minutes later Barbara asked if anyone was ready for dessert.

'I'm ready for presents,' Michael said, giddy with excitement. 'Who brought gold?'

Ira kept eating.

In February Pa came home from the hospital with his puffers and stool softeners. He was staying with Sheldon and me and the boys. He was angry that I had thrown away his long underwear, dirtied in the emergency room. But the first few days went well. Neither the pain nor the bloody urine had come back. I was happy. I loved him. I wanted him to eat. He was warm and comfortable, set up in Harry's room next to Sheldon's home office. All his medicines were on Harry's nightstand.

Under the *Where the Wild Things Are* poster he nested like an old bird. He pulled the Blue Jays coverlet up to his chin. All around him were Harry's collections, a shelf of autographed baseballs, plastic boxes filled with hockey cards and marbles.

Harry wanted to move to the basement, but Pa said, 'Who sleeps in a basement? A pauper sleeps in a basement.' So Harry set up a mattress at the foot of our bed. Pa told his friends he was being treated like a god. 'I'm treated like royalty,' Pa said when his friends called. 'A king or a viscount.' He spoke about living five years; he spoke about living five months. Davey figured that he had cut down on his smoking by three hundred percent.

Most of the day he slept. But as soon as he came in the door from school, Harry asked 'How's Pa?' and went to wake him up. He told Pa about things he was reading in the *Guinness Book of World Records*, about a man who had bitten a light bulb and swallowed it down with Windex. And a woman who sniffed in a popcorn kernel and pushed it out a corner of her eye. They watched television shows together in the late afternoon. Skill testing for dogs. Texas prison escapes. *The Simpsons*, Harry's favourite. But nothing took precedence over Pa's bowel movement. Each day I wanted to know what Pa had to eat and if he'd had his stool. Pa was quick to oblige. 'Sheldon made me my breakfast. I had grits – what I call a kasha. With milk and sugar. I had a tea, a glass of apple juice. I had a normal breakfast.' He paused at the summit. 'And then I had my own stomach. The stool was almost perfect.'

I watched Sheldon being kind to his father. His touch was tender and careful. Sometimes Sheldon didn't bother getting dressed in the morning. He wore his bathrobe all day long because someone had to stay around the house with Pa.

On the second Tuesday Pa said gloomily, 'I haven't had my stool. And I vomited.' Maybe a daily bowel movement is a thing of the past,

I thought. 'And there was blood in the pee. A long string of blood.'

I put a down comforter over him and then I opened a window. He liked the fresh air. Usually I left the window open for seven minutes. 'Let me read to you,' I said. I had been meaning to read to him some Yiddish stories, especially Peretz's 'If Not Higher', the story of a kind rabbi who does good deeds during the Days of Awe. '"Early Friday morning, at the time of the Penitential Prayers, the Rabbi of Nemirov would vanish,"' I began.

The air was cold, but there was no wind in the room. Pa closed his eyes. He seemed to be sleeping. '"He was nowhere to be seen – neither in the synagogue nor in the two Houses of Study nor at a minyan."'

I got up and closed the window. 'Should I keep reading?' I asked. 'Would you like me to keep going?'

Pa struggled to sit up in bed. 'I told you to buy me a card for Michael. And a beautiful card,' he said gruffly. 'I want to put a hundred dollars in it. I didn't like being at his house without a present.' Pa had to lie back down. 'Michael cancelled his fishing trip. He's a good son.'

Grimly I continued to read. '"The rabbi, long life to him, enters the wood."' Pa burped, groaned, drifted off to sleep.

After dinner while we were cleaning up, I said to Sheldon, 'I'm not buying a card for Michael. If you want, you can buy a card.' Then I listed all my married friends who had very little contact with their husbands' side of the family.

It was time for *Wheel of Fortune*. We gathered in the living room. A pillow and a comforter were brought down from upstairs. Pa stretched out on the couch. The kids sat on the floor. Sheldon figured out FORMICA COUNTERTOPS and Pa said to me, 'Your husband has a quick mind.' Harry smiled proudly and Pa closed his eyes. When Pa woke up, we were already watching *Jeopardy*.

'I saw God,' Pa said.

'Turn down the TV,' I said. 'Pa saw God.'

'Was he on a mountain?' Sheldon asked. 'Give us the details.'

'Don't interrupt,' I said, leaning forward.

'He was in heaven.'

'High in the sky?' Sheldon wanted to know.

'He was up there. I told you. Above the clouds. And not alone.'

'Who was there?' Sheldon pressed. 'Who was with him? Allah? Jesus? All One?'

'What did God look like?' Harry said.

'Shh, shh,' said Pa. 'How can I tell you? How can I explain? What do you want me to say? A Hasidic Jew with side curls?'

Harry started to cry.

'No, Harry. It's been a great life,' Pa said, enjoying his mystic role. 'It's not a tragedy to die in your eighties. You can't live forever. And I don't want to suffer.' He folded a tissue and wiped his watering eyes. 'It's not good to be sick. You can't drive or live like a mensch. You don't feel like yourself.'

Then Davey started to cry.

Pa said, 'You boys are crying for nothing. This is life. I want to go home. I want to take a bath in mine own tub. Come with me if you want.'

Pa burped and farted. I told Davey to run out for Tums. Pa's stomach was upset. I felt terrible. I'd overfed him at dinner.

In the last year Pa had befriended a number of Polish women in his neighbourhood who took care of the Jewish elderly. He had put the word out on his own behalf that he needed someone. For ten dollars more a week Elenka came to Pa from an old man with Alzheimer's who lived right around the block.

Now Elenka answered the door. She was a pretty woman with copper red hair and a turned-up nose. Her eyes were a beautiful shade of yellowish brown.

'She keeps herself constantly busy,' Pa said with pride. 'She doesn't slow down. All day long she finds something to do. Until ten o'clock last night she kept working. I told her to rest. I can't get her to quit.

'She's making all the foods I ate as a boy,' Pa went on. 'I had riga sprouts with mayonnaise and onions for lunch. Delicious. And tonight she fed me borscht and mashed potatoes. Just the right amount. Not too much. All natural ingredients.'

Elenka smiled deferentially. It turned out she was exactly my age – forty-six. She was probably a doctor or a lawyer or a government official in the old country, I thought.

I said, 'Elenka, you're a real find. Pa's luck is unbelievable. Too good to be true.'

Pa talked as if Elenka were unable to understand a word of English. 'She's already engaged to a truck driver,' he said. 'She needs his papers to stay in Canada.'

Elenka took off her rubber gloves. She went into the kitchen and plugged in the teakettle. I followed her, got out four mugs, put some lemon cookies on a plate. Together we brought in the tea. Sheldon helped Pa to the dining room.

'She's divorced,' Pa said while Elenka nibbled on a cookie. 'Her husband was a rough bastard. He beat her up.' Pa's gaunt face was bright. 'The truck driver is what I don't like. He wants to pick her up on Friday and take her to Montreal for the weekend.'

'Everyone wants time off,' I said. 'Everyone needs a break.'

Pa said, 'I'll give her one day and one night. But not two days and two nights. I won't tolerate it.' He hit the table with his fist. 'I don't want to take a dime away from Sheldon and Michael.'

'Calm down, Pa,' Sheldon said. 'You're being unreasonable.'

Pa started to shout. 'You don't understand. If she goes away, I'll find someone else. I don't want to spend the money! No, I won't pay.'

'Forget all this,' I said to Pa. 'You're upsetting yourself. Eat now. While you have the appetite.' I pushed the plate of cookies towards him.

'Would you like a glass of juice?' Elenka said, and went into the kitchen.

'She won't stick around if you act like a pharaoh,' I hissed. 'Why would she?'

'Take it easy, Pa,' Sheldon whispered. 'She's doing her best. She's perfect. Don't blow it.'

'I hope it will work out in your favour,' Elenka said quietly. She had returned with a small glass of apple juice. 'I'll try to persuade him.'

I looked at Sheldon. Usually he held something against the Poles for the history of anti-Semitism was always on his mind. But with Elenka he was a model of forgiveness, nodding like a cow.

'Thank you,' Pa said. He took the glass from Elenka and began to drink.

On Friday night Sheldon dropped me off around seven o'clock. I had volunteered to spend the night at Pa's.

Elenka was ready to leave by the time I arrived. She looked even prettier than she had several days before. Her overnight bag was waiting by the door. She was wearing make-up.

'You look really great,' I said.

'Thanks,' said Elenka and went downstairs to watch TV.

We waited for the truck driver. Several times the phone rang for Elenka; it was he, providing up-to-the-minute news of his whereabouts. Then I would call Sheldon to relay the information. Even Davey and Harry wanted to know where this guy was and when he was coming. 'He's just called from outside of London,' I said. 'He should be here in an hour.'

I washed the dinner dishes and made Pa his evening snack. I gave him his medicines. By ten o'clock he looked like he would keel over from exhaustion. But still he refused to lie down on the sofa or go upstairs to sleep.

'I'll lock up when Elenka leaves,' I said. 'That's why I'm here.'

'I'll do it!' Pa snapped. 'I don't need you!'

I didn't bother to argue. Finally, at midnight, a horn honked, one sonorous blast, and a white truck, almost half a block long, pulled up in front of Pa's house. I helped Pa get up. Like little jungle monkeys we parted branches, peering out over the tangle of tropical trees that were lined up in front of the living-room window. (Their cultivation was one of Pa's hobbies.) I tried to make out the driver in the cab of the truck. I supposed he was handsome. He didn't cut the engine.

'I need someone here all the time,' Pa said to Elenka as she buttoned up her wool overcoat. 'Explain it to him.'

'Twenty-four seven,' I said meekly. 'Or thereabouts. That's our dilemma.'

Elenka stood by the door. 'I'll try to make it come out in your favour,' she said, picking up her suitcase. 'Goodbye.'

We watched her step out into the snow like Lara to Zhivago.

'Tonight she'll sleep inside the truck. There's a little cabin,' Pa said. 'He'll go all the way to Montreal without stopping. That's how he makes a living.'

I brought Pa upstairs to bed. I tucked him in. Then I retired to the room where Sheldon had slept when he was a university student. It was the smallest of three bedrooms and in dire need of a paint job. The walls were marked and dirty and gave me an utter and loathsome feeling of despair. Last year, at this time, I had tried to convince Pa to hire the nice young man who was painting our kitchen. The painter's bid was aboveboard and reasonable, but Pa hadn't wanted to spend the money.

An hour passed and I couldn't shake off the pervasive sense of desperation. There was virtually nothing of interest to read on the bookshelf but I'd brought a magazine with me. So I got up out of bed and tried to fashion a night table out of a rickety plant stand. I set it up next to the bed, but the cord on the lamp was far too short and wouldn't stretch back across the room to the one electrical socket under the window. The fact that the lamp was without a shade only depressed me further, but I hoped that reading would make me drowsy. At the same time, I knew I'd never find an extension cord at this time of night and I didn't want to go wandering and searching through the dark house.

Besides, I was cold. My blanket was flimsy and tattered. Everything here was ugly and broken and cheap and old. An acoustic guitar with all its strings snapped hung on a nail over the dresser, as it had for twenty-one years, since I'd been married to Sheldon.

All night long the dining-room wall clock rang out every quarter hour. In his room Pa was restless and groaning. How could anyone sleep in this place? What was I trying to prove? Of course somebody needed to stay with the old man. Someone had to look after him at all times. But now all my efforts seemed doomed and useless. The empty bookshelf, the broken guitar, the bare light bulb, and Pa's snoring were like a configuration of symbols, fragments of a dream, incongruous objects in a painting by de Chirico, from which I could fathom no meaning. What does all this dutifulness say about me? I asked myself. What am I doing in this creaky old bed?

I'd acted like this before. When I first met Sheldon, I brought Pa out on all of our dates. If we went to the movies, Pa came. If we had friends for dinner, Pa was invited. If we went to the theatre, Pa got the aisle seat. He even joined us on vacations. Still, it was obvious that Pa would never love me the way he loved Sheldon and Michael. For one thing, I couldn't say a bad word about them. Even as a joke. He wouldn't allow it. They were perfect. He had survived so that they could be born.

And I didn't have *yichis*. He'd met my father and couldn't deny I came from the rags and cinders side of the tracks. In our wedding pictures, I could see how Pa's face had collapsed in misgiving when we made our vows.

Finally Sheldon had said, 'Enough is enough. I don't want Pa to go everywhere with us any more.'

'But we're married,' I said.

'Most people don't have a chaperone once they're married. They want to be independent.'

'Don't you love your father?' I had argued.

'Sure, I love my father. But I don't want him in my pocket.'

Now I was thinking how desperate I had been. Pa was the most reliable person I'd ever known. A hundred times more reliable than Sheldon. No matter what the circumstances, he never let you down. He had never despised me.

Some women with a father like mine fell romantically in love with an older man, one in a position of power or authority, at least for a time. But I'd skipped that fate.

Life had offered me the experience of Pa. Pa was my chance to explore the territory of having a father. Of being a daughter. Otherwise I would have missed out on that great adventure. I had forged interaction. I'd created a bond. *Oh, reason not the need.* Pa wasn't a feast, but he wasn't a famine.

I pictured Sheldon at home, warm and comfy, the dog curled up at the end of the bed. The clock rang out. I tossed and turned, and passed the night thinking about all the strange obligations that I called love.

Over the weekend a carousel of caretakers went in and out of Pa's house. Sheldon came over as well as Michael and Barbara and their children. Rebecca ran through the house, opening drawers and cabinets and rummaging around for things to play with. She made discoveries. A set of carved wooden birds that sat on the piano, a plastic elephant with one tusk that had been a decanter for men's cologne, and Sheldon's broken guitar, which she hauled up and down the stairs. Pa was beside himself for her touching his things; he never stopped complaining about her touching his things. 'She'll break something! She'll steal!' But he hadn't the energy to stop her and no one paid him any heed. At the kitchen table Sheldon read Primo Levi's *Moments of Reprieve*, the book left behind the week before by the volunteer sent over from Jewish Home and Palliative Care. Davey talked on the phone with his friends. Harry, Holly and Rory watched TV.

On Saturday afternoon Melissa gave Pa a manicure which cheered him. He called her 'a family girl' for the first time in six years. Rebecca unscrewed the plastic elephant's head from its body, long empty of cologne, and waved the bottle neck under Pa's nose. Pa sat up and sniffed. Even smelling made him weary. Still, it was something to do.

Everyone was waiting for Elenka to arrive. On Sunday night it was getting late and Pa was tired. Barbara made some phone calls to trace her and all of a sudden Elenka gave her a hundred excuses. She was stuck in a snowstorm; she'd been poisoned by food. She was staying in Montreal. But by midnight no one cared what became of Elenka, not even me, and Barbara had stopped calling her. She was going into hospital. She was flying to Mars. We barely wished her well. We didn't wish her well.

At first I had tried to defend her. 'She doesn't have a car. She doesn't have much money. Maybe something bad happened with the truck driver? But soon I gave up. I could tell Pa was disappointed. I felt sorry for him.

'She said she was going to try to have it work out in my favour,' he kept saying.

When she had hung up the last time, Barbara said, 'I knew she was a prima donna without a work ethic,' and she went to Elenka's room, packed her things and carted a box out to the porch. We never saw Elenka again. She never came back. Eventually another Polish woman who worked in the neighbourhood came around to pick up her stuff.

Because Barbara was used to hiring people (she'd always had help in the house), the job of choosing Pa's next caregiver fell to her. She found Mimi through an ad in the paper.

The day after Mimi was hired I went to meet her at Pa's house. Mimi stood behind the door as she opened it, letting it swing back into the front hall so that she was momentarily hidden. Then she sprang out like a Jack-in-the-box. She was tall and buxom. Her hair stuck out wildly in all directions as if the ends had been singed by fire. She wore tight yellow jeans and a tight pink sweater. She'd dotted the blemishes on her dark face with a thick, white ointment. She said she was twenty-seven years old.

Pa looked even bonier than when I'd seen him a day ago. He sat hunched over at the kitchen table, complaining that no one came to visit him and that Mimi didn't know how to cook. She didn't even know how to follow the written instructions on a package of instant oatmeal. She puzzled over rice. For lunch she'd made a salt soup with chicken parts, a perfect waste of food for a man who had lived three days off one potato in Siberia. Why hadn't he heard from me? Where had I been? What was I doing? It was late.

'But Mimi's here,' I said.

'She isn't good. I try to tell her how to make food. But she's a nincompoop.'

'Never mind,' I said. I had brought over a bag full of groceries. I handed Mimi a jar of split pea soup and she opened it at the counter. She held her nose, screwed up her face, and emptied the entire contents into a saucepan. Then she turned on the stove, holding the little pot at arm's length as she put it on the front burner.

'Hurry up with that soup,' Pa said in a bark. 'I'm hungry. It's hot already. Just give it to me.' He turned around laboriously and glared at us both. He thinks I'm a nincompoop, too, I thought. I took out a bowl from the kitchen cabinet, handed it to Mimi, and she poured the soup from the saucepan into the bowl. Then she brought the bowl to the table and slapped it down in front of Pa.

Pa looked at the bowl of soup. 'I can't eat all this,' he yelled. 'Don't you see I'm a sick old man?'

Mimi shrugged her shoulders. She picked up the bowl and spilled some of the soup out into the kitchen sink. Then she plunked the bowl back onto the table and Pa bent over and began to eat noisily. I gave Mimi a complicit smile. I knew Pa was a difficult old man. Let us now praise old difficult men! But Mimi didn't smile back. Sullenly she picked up the *Star* from the kitchen table. Then she went into the dining room with the portable phone.

'Give her a chance,' I said quietly. 'It's only the second day. In a while the two of you will get acquainted. These things take time.'

Pa shook his head and blew on his spoon. 'I'll never get used,' he said. 'She's stupid as a foot. I have to tell her, "This is a cup. This is a saucer." She hasn't heard of cantaloupe or cereal.'

'Yeah, I like kids,' I overheard Mimi say. 'I have lots of experience. I was a teacher in my country. I love kids.'

I found her poring over the want ads with a pink magic marker.

'Why don't you give it a few days?' I said when she put down the phone. 'These things take time. In a while the two of you will get acquainted.' I wondered if Mimi already hated Pa.

'She needs the money,' Pa hollered from the kitchen. 'If she wants to stay in this country and earn money, she has to work.' He started to burp.

I went back to the kitchen, helped Pa to his feet, and walked him into the living room where he had set up camp by the long velvet sofa.

There he kept his Kleenex box, a wastebasket, and a bunch of old cassettes that Harry had found in the front hall credenza. Sheldon had put a tape recorder on the coffee table so that Pa could listen to the radio or books on tape. I fluffed his pillow and covered him with a blanket.

'She eats like a horse,' Pa said. 'She never had it so good.'

'Let her eat, Pa,' I said. 'What do you care?'

'She never served the chicken. She ate it all up herself.'

'She's hungry. So what?' I smiled at Mimi.

'And she goes through the shelves. That's how she found the chocolate powder.'

'Did you have milk? Milk is good, Pa. Calcium for the bones.'

'She's stubborn, too. Can't remember to close a door, a cupboard, a drawer. You can hit your head.'

'Closing is an easy skill to learn,' I said. Even I can close, I thought.

'And last night she went to the back of the house. I didn't have the strength to follow her out there.'

I turned to Mimi.

'I'm dying in here,' Mimi said. 'He wants me cooped up all the time. I need fresh air.'

'That's kinda the job,' I said. 'Didn't Barbara explain? You're supposed to look after him. Like a companion.' Casually I tried to give Mimi a few helpful hints.

I explained rice and bread and small helpings of vegetables and fruit. Tomorrow I could tackle complex carbohydrates. 'We want to make sure that Pa eats a combination of foods,' I said. 'I don't mind shopping. I can do most of the cooking, too. But you must watch out that he doesn't fall. Especially on the staircase.'

Mimi made a face and drew another wide pink circle.

'Let's try to make a go of it,' I said. She won't last two more days, I thought. Then I began to ask Mimi about herself.

She put down the magic marker, got up, and came into the living room. She sat down in one of the high-back chairs and said that her father had died of black magic. 'An *obeah* killed him.'

'Like voodoo?' I asked. 'A hex?'

Mimi nodded. Her white spots looked exotic. 'Some people are envious,' she said. 'They think what you have is bigger and they want it. A demon came and my father went crazy. He fell down dead.'

'How do you know?' I said. 'Who told you?' Are you hearing this, Pa? I wondered. Mimi is a real person, too. I wanted Pa to know.

'My mother told me,' said Mimi. 'All the time I was asking my mother what happened to my daddy.'

Pa raised his head. 'Leave her alone,' he said hoarsely. 'I'm not well.' He wants the attention back, I thought. I was getting to know him like a daughter.

Pa said, 'If she doesn't have a father, don't be harsh. What do I eat, anyway? It's not a matter of eating. Let her be.'

Good Pa, sparing the fatherless children.

In less than a week there was a new congeniality between Pa and Mimi. On a Wednesday afternoon, she answered the door in a conventional manner. Pa was sitting up on the sofa, burping and looking like the elderly Picasso, clean and spiffy. Mimi had bathed him, and cut his eyebrows, nose hair and fingernails. He was wearing grey sweat pants and a dark blue turtleneck that I had never seen before. I dropped my grocery bags in the front hall and went to sit down on the settee with them in the living room.

'You look good, Pa,' I said. 'Very nice.'

Mimi grinned. 'The nurse said I rubbed Pa's feet so well that they're circulating.'

'Pa's lucky to have you.'

'And how!' said Pa. 'You wouldn't believe what a modern hippie she is. A wild cat in the desert. She's crazy about boys. Boys are all she thinks about.'

Mimi and Pa had obviously had some conversations. I saw this as a good sign. I smiled at them both.

Then Mimi called me into the kitchen where we could talk privately. 'Michael wants to poison Pa,' Mimi said in a low voice. 'He's giving him four or five of the blue pills when he comes over at night.'

'Those are over-the-counter pills for flatulence,' I said. 'For gas. The same as I've been giving Pa the gripe water.' Then I felt forced to say, 'Michael wouldn't hurt Pa.' But part of me was glad that someone else had suspicions about him.

Now Mimi said she didn't need any time off. She was willing to work round the clock and even offering to do a little housework. Nor was food any longer an issue. Pa was sending Mimi up the block for prepared foods – gefilte fish, schnitzel, chopped liver and blintzes – and telling her to buy whatever she wanted, even beef patties for midnight snacks. His appetite was way down but he enjoyed watching her eat.

A routine had developed. In the morning Pa slept in and came down late for his breakfast. Then he rested on the sofa for a bit, took his medications and went back up for a nap. In the afternoon, after lunch, Pa lay on the sofa and Mimi stretched out on the floor beside him. Together they would doze or listen to a book on tape.

'Yesterday I couldn't wake her up for love or money,' Pa said fondly, his hands pillowed under his head. 'The phone was ringing. Wake up! Wake up! But she was out cold. Like a bear in hibernation. Sleepyhead! Sleepyhead!'

Mimi grinned and gazed at Pa with affection. She clicked on the tape recorder and curled up at Pa's feet while I went to put the groceries away in the kitchen. They had been listening to the story of Kirk Douglas's life, *A Ragpicker's Son*, which Michael had borrowed from the library. I heard Kirk Douglas talking about his engagement to a young, immature starlet in Paris. He said he had an older, even more wonderful girlfriend in Cannes. 'You can imagine how beautiful those two weeks were,' Kirk Douglas said.

'Those Hollywood men lived a good, unbelievable life,' said Pa. 'Like princes and kings and dukes.' He began to cough loudly and I went to check on him. He was sitting up and flapping his hands.

'We should scare him for the hiccups,' Mimi said. 'Or take a thread, spit on the end, wrap it up and stick it on his forehead.' Her ear was bent to the tape recorder.

Pa shook his head and chopped on the back of his neck with the side of his hand. 'Alleyoop,' he roared, and lay back down on the sofa, exhausted.

Mimi turned off the tape recorder. 'Do you want to watch television now?' she asked. But Pa was no longer interested in television, not in the Leafs, or the Bills, or the new President of the United States. He didn't care that hoof and mouth disease was poisoning all the livestock in Northern Ireland.

After Mimi left the room, Pa said, 'She's already proposed marriage to me. I said, "Why do you want to marry me? I'm an old man." And then she intentionally rubbed her big breast against my arm. A coquette. She wants my citizenship.'

A week later Mimi went out. When she didn't return, Pa called Michael and Barbara. Then he called Sheldon and me. The family convened in the living room. Davey and Harry came too.

'She's four hours late,' Pa said. 'She said she'd be home at one-thirty. It's already six. I bet she's been arrested.'

Mimi arrived at seven o'clock. She was dressed in a smart black waist jacket and knee-high black boots. Her hair was done up with a scarf in the design of the Confederate flag.

'I'm leaving,' she said. 'I came for my things.'

'Where were you?' I said. 'We were worried. Pa was alone all afternoon.'

Mimi glared at all of us. 'I have a life.'

'What life?' Michael said. 'You're fired. Get out.'

'She was out with the boys,' Pa said. 'Always a boy. She has one in every corner of the city. I tried to forbid her.'

'You have no right to forbid her,' I said.

Harry asked incredulously, 'Does Pa like Mimi?'

'Shh,' I said. 'He's allowed.'

'That's gross,' said Davey. 'Really gross.'

Barbara rolled her eyes. She also disapproved of Pa's fondness for young women. 'You won't get a reference from me,' she said.

Davey went over to Mimi and pointed at her scarf. 'You're wearing the Rebel flag,' he said. 'To a lot of black people, that flag means slavery. If I were you I'd take it off.'

Mimi touched her head, unconvinced. 'I don't care. I like the pattern. It's pretty.' For the first time she glanced at Pa and smiled. The prince, the king, the duke! He was on the sofa, a befuddled, tired, sick old man waiting to be folded into a quilt. He didn't look like the elderly Picasso any more. His bathrobe and pyjamas needed changing. 'Let her go,' he said. 'Let her leave.'

I was sorry to see Mimi go. I liked Mimi. I had thought Mimi's concern for Pa was real. I considered Mimi a friend and wanted to help her find a good dermatologist. I went to stand in the kitchen with a pain gnawing in my chest. I could not say goodbye.

March was cold. Thick snowflakes drifted through the air. Outside the boys chipped away at ice. Pa was incredibly tired and didn't want to come down for breakfast. Sheldon was short-tempered; he stayed in his office, photocopying and faxing and talking on the phone. When Pa got up around nine o'clock, he made loud farting noises in the bathroom. I waited for him in the hallway to help him down the stairs. 'How are you, Pa?' I said.

'Fine, thank you. I don't think it's warm outside. But it's warm in here.'

I made fresh coffee and served him bits of things – a bit of oatmeal, a bit of bagel, a bit of sliced pear. I gave him two bits of mandel bread, and then took one off his plate. Sheldon came down and peeled an apple. Pa ate a few pieces. Then I put nine grapes into a small bowl and Pa said angrily, 'I will not eat them!' I had bought pineapple, had thought while I stood in the checkout line that this might be the last time Pa would taste pineapple. I had forgotten to put it on the table and now I didn't bother.

His face was haggard. I smiled at him. He shook his head and smiled a little; he was withering away. In the *Times* there was a story about Mormons, which Sheldon read out loud. So for a while we made fun of polygamists being chased out of Ohio. Then Pa gave his usual lecture on the fact that Jesus was a Jew and the Romans were his crucifiers.

'Come, Pa,' I said. 'I'll set you up in front of the TV.'

Pa watched Harry's ABBA video and then he went upstairs for his bowel movement.

'You're happy you had your stomach,' I said. I was waiting for him outside the bathroom so that I could walk him to his bed.

'And how!' Pa said, beaming. 'You're right!'

After he rested for a while Sheldon gave him his bath. Then I cleaned off the flakes of dead skin that stuck to the sides of the tub. 'Did he kiss you, Shelley?' I asked. 'Did Pa give you a kiss?'

Sheldon resignedly met my eye. 'Yes, he kissed me.'

Around the house Pa carried his leather billfold with the hundred dollars allotted to him by Michael. The wallet was falling apart, held together by an old elastic band. After Harry got him upstairs, Pa would sometimes try to give Harry five dollars and Harry would start to cry. All this took a lot of time. Pa would slowly reach his hand into his bathrobe pocket. He would take out the wallet, undo the rubber band, open the wallet, choose the five-dollar bill, close the wallet back up, replace the rubber band, and return the wallet to his bathrobe pocket. Then he would lie down on the bed.

Harry's tears came quick.

One afternoon Pa told me, 'I want you to have my car. I've told Sheldon already. And Michael agrees. He has enough cars.'

'No, Pa, no,' I said. 'I don't want your car. In the spring, you'll go driving. We'll go for a ride.'

He considered. 'Maybe. Who knows?' And then he fell asleep.

On a Friday Michael closed Pa's US dollar account. He became suspicious because two hundred and seventy five dollars was missing, and Pa was too frightened to tell him that a few years ago he had bought Israeli bonds for Davey and Harry. That afternoon Michael came over and yelled at Pa about the missing money. 'Where is it? Where is it?' he wanted to know.

Pa hunkered down in the armchair. 'Sheldon borrowed it,' he said. 'He forgot to pay me back.'

'Pa's getting foggy,' Michael said triumphantly. 'Especially around numbers.'

I took Sheldon into the kitchen. 'This is between you and your father and Michael. I'm not getting involved.'

'I already gave Michael the money. He wanted it back. I wrote him a cheque.'

My throat tightened. 'The money that Pa gave your children as a gift?'

Sheldon paused. 'Michael always got more than I did. A car, an engagement ring, a sports shirt, a basement renovation. He wasn't afraid to ask. How do you think he got to be a millionaire?'

I took out dessert plates and cups and saucers for tea. 'Pa's alive,' I said. 'I don't think it's right to make requests.' Then I asked, 'Does Michael hate you?'

'I got a lot of attention when I had rheumatic fever. I spent almost a year in hospital.'

'You were six years old. You think he still hates you for that?'

'Not hates. I don't think he thinks he ever got enough attention. And he never liked sharing.' Sheldon sighed. 'I think he resents Pa. Isn't this about Pa? Pa used to bang his own head against the wall. Literally.'

'He never got over being the sole survivor,' I said sadly. 'How could he? Too much anger. Too much pain and guilt. Not one living relative.'

'It really is biblical,' Sheldon said. 'Now Pa's the dying patriarch.'

I carried out a bowl of oranges. Sheldon brought the pot of tea. Barbara was sitting on the couch next to the dog.

'Michael says Pa's lost it,' Barbara said. I watched Barbara petting the dog and cooing into her ear. She had a big heart for animals. She took in a lot of strays. They had a lot of pets and vet bills.

In bed that night Sheldon did some imitations of Pa's grunts and moans to cheer me up. He mimicked the way Pa cocked his head sideways when he took his daily tablespoons of Lactulose. His impersonations were good. We laughed.

'What is it that you're reading?' Sheldon asked.

'"So on receiving the news of Ivan Ilych's death,"' I read, '"the first thought of each of the gentlemen in that private room was of the changes and promotions it might occasion among themselves or their acquaintances. And as Vinnikov and Shtabel thought of their appointments and promotions, it was impossible not to think of their gain."'

Sheldon turned off the light.

The next morning Pa said, 'I want you to go over to my house and take the sugar. A long time ago I stocked up when there was a sale. I don't need to report everything to Michael. He says I owe him fifteen hundred dollars. I said, "Show me." And I want some money in my pocket. I don't play cards. I don't run around with women. I don't throw it out the window.'

In the afternoon Sheldon and I lugged twenty-five kilos of sugar out of Pa's house.

'We could bake a hundred cakes,' I said. 'There's enough sugar here for four or five years. Maybe ten.'

Sheldon was ragged and depressed. 'I hope we live that long,' he said.

At first Pa wanted no part of Joyce-Ann because she was sixty. But Joyce-Ann was the only one who answered the ad Barbara put in the *Star* and who fit the criteria of six days a week at two hundred and fifty dollars. Joyce-Ann was a small, thin woman who was being treated for carpal tunnel syndrome in her left hand.

'She's an old lady,' Pa said. 'She won't be able to lift me. If I fell she wouldn't be able to do a thing.'

During the day Joyce-Ann wore a housedress and slippers. Pa didn't find her pretty to look at. 'She's small and ugly,' he complained. 'Her teeth are buck.'

But Joyce-Ann needed the money. 'Yes, Pa,' she'd say. 'Yes, Pa.'

In early April, Harry and I drove up to Pa's house at one o'clock on a Saturday afternoon. The magnolia in the front yard was budding. We found Pa heaving in the kitchen chair. Joyce-Ann was puttering at the sink.

'How's Pa?' I asked.

'I'm worse,' Pa said.

'Not in any way worse.' Joyce-Ann said. 'Yesterday the nurse was here and gave him his enema. The vital signs were good.'

Pa shook his head despairingly.

'Pa ate a good lunch today, didn't you, Pa?' Joyce-Ann said. 'It's good that you're here.'

Pa held up his hands and rolled his eyes like he hated Joyce-Ann. 'I'm not dying,' he said. 'As long as I don't have pains.'

'You're grouchy today, Pa,' I said. 'You're in a bad mood.'

'You can say what you want. I'll tell you like it is.'

'Your voice is reedy,' I said. 'I wonder if you've caught cold.'

'Maybe,' Joyce-Ann said balefully.

'I don't understand why I'm so tired,' Pa said, hanging his head.

'C'mon, Pa,' said Joyce-Ann. 'Let's get you back to bed.' Pa had no choice but to lean into Harry and Joyce-Ann. The procession moved slowly. I called the doctor.

'We should get an elevator so that Pa can ride up and down the stairs,' Harry said.

'It's not worth it,' said Pa.

'Yes, it is,' Harry said. 'Yes, it is.'

Harry and I stayed the afternoon. Around three-thirty Doctor Kirshen examined Pa in his bedroom.

'The cancer in the kidney is from the lung,' the doctor said. 'This means it's a secondary primary. And not a primary secondary. It's slow growing.'

He tapped around with his fingers on Pa's chest and abdomen. He listened to his heart with a stethoscope.

Pa said, 'I could live like this. If it doesn't get worse than this.'

'Looking good,' said Dr Kirshen to Pa. 'Still looking good.'

I found this hard to believe. There was barely anything left of Pa. His was a daily suffering. The flesh falling away from the bones, the constant sleep, the mischief in the pants. He was besieged. From the inside out he was eaten alive. He was almost a skeleton.

When we were out in the hallway, I said, 'Does he have pneumonia? He's wheezing.'

Dr Kirshen nodded. 'You'll have to make the decision about penicillin.'

'Of course, we want penicillin,' I said. I didn't care how old Pa was. I didn't care if he was an infant, or a teenager, or the young mother of twins. 'Let's start him on it right away.' Then I realized that the doctor hesitated because of the instructions: Do not resuscitate. But Pa wasn't dying of pneumonia. I didn't see how those instructions applied.

Dr Kirshen wrote the prescription and handed it to me. He warned me against burnout. He mentioned that his first wife had died of cancer. 'Let the nurse bathe your father-in-law,' he said. 'Let the caretaker do the shopping and cook.' Then he suggested peer counselling from the cancer support centre. 'There are people out there who've been through this before,' he said. 'And they know how to help. They want to help. Let them help.'

Dear Peer, I thought, *I'm tired and frightened. And I may end up petty and bitter. About Michael and Barbara and money and things I don't really care about. I'm grieving and Pa isn't even dead. I admit I need help. Does grief ever end?*

Now it seemed that Sheldon was getting stoned as much as he could. 'The only pleasure I have,' Sheldon said, 'is getting high.' We were walking the dog on a Friday evening and Sheldon was smoking up in the ravine near our house.

It was early spring, not yet dusk. The trees were filling with leaves. The dog ran ahead of us. She lay down in puddles.

'Freud said we get depressed when confronted with impermanence,' I told Sheldon. 'Or we devalue what we see and push it away. You can't love if you're already mourning your losses.'

'Oh, yeah,' Sheldon said and took a deep puff on his joint. He had given Pa his bath that afternoon and shaved him.

'The Buddha points out that life is actually a state of constant decay. What you want is a mind that neither clings nor rejects. Ideally transience should be enlightening. Each exhalation is a little mini-death.'

Sheldon laughed. I could tell he was getting enlightened. Earlier in the week Pa had shown me his bedsores. He had wanted me to look. His emaciation was stark and unbridled. 'This is a hard time,' I said to Sheldon. 'Maybe meditation would help.'

'I'm not interested in meditation. I couldn't do it. I hate the idea of sitting quietly for an hour with my eyes closed. I'd rather watch TV.'

I looked him in the face. His eyes had narrowed into slits. So I asked, 'How did it go today? How was Pa's bath? Did he like his shave? Was he grateful? Did he kiss you?'

Sheldon took another toke. 'If you wouldn't mind,' he said, expelling the smoke. 'Not to ask any more questions.' He gritted his teeth. 'The kissing is over.'

Now we were spending most of our time in Pa's bedroom. Barbara wanted Pa to get out of bed to use the bathroom. 'He should sit up,' she said. 'He should walk.'

'Sit up, Pa,' Michael said. 'Pull yourself up.'

Michael brought over Rebecca's stool so that Pa could swing his legs from the bed and onto it before he stepped down on the carpet.

'What does it matter?' I said. 'You're insisting on strength that's no longer available. He could fall and hit his head. Let him rest.' It sickened me when Pa tried to oblige them.

But the end was near. It didn't matter any more what Pa desired or whom he was trying to please. He needed help to the bathroom. Only ten feet from the bed and it seemed like a hundred miles. He may have used the step stool once. Then all of a sudden his bed was too hard. The purple velvet bedspread, once a vestige of his wife's royal taste, no longer felt plush or soft on his body. It was just a piece of fabric folded over a mattress that seemed as hard as a plank of wood. Likewise the sheets felt rough. The blankets were coarse and the pillows too high and uncomfortable.

Then Home Care provided an air bed for Pa. At first the circulating air was a source of comfort. 'The bed is talking,' Pa said to me. 'There's music. And plays. Shakespeare. I feel like I'm resting on feathers. I enjoy it!' But soon the bed became a dissatisfaction. Pa said he couldn't feel the air move any more; in the middle of the night he called Michael and woke the family. Rebecca couldn't fall back to sleep.

That afternoon Michael called Sheldon.

Sheldon reported, 'Michael says, "Pa is demanding. He's spoiled." Michael's growing impatient,' Sheldon said to me. 'Pa's a liability. It's taking him a long time to die.'

None of it mattered. Pa *was* dying. The old friends came, the ones whom Pa had put off with his temper, angered with his opinions, infuriated with his putdowns and criticisms. All of a sudden his elderly friends looked muscular and robust. I put my arm around Pa as if to shield him from their thoughts. But he didn't need my defence. No subject held his interest. Not wealth, not news, not the Spielberg Holocaust Project.

He did want to know the details of Solly Wertzer's death. But Solly's widow, Miri, wouldn't tell him, holding back something precious. I could never forget how Miri threw herself on Solly's coffin. *Oy gevalt. Too soon. Too soon.*

'I don't need her barley soup,' Pa said when Miri left. 'It's not the best I ever tasted.'

'Do you want to die, Pa?' Michael asked him. 'Are you ready to die?'

Feebly Pa shook his head. 'No, I'll carry on like this. As long as I don't have pains.'

But Pa was making accidents on the way to the toilet; the mischief in his pants was becoming less rare.

'Pa made mischief in his pants again,' Joyce-Ann would say. 'Time to start talking about diapers.'

'No!' Pa snarled like a pygmy tyrant.

The transition wasn't easy.

'Do you have any surprises for me today?' Joyce-Anne would say. Pa would say, 'When my mind goes, I'll tell you.'

'Yes, Pa.'

I had hoped for good-natured concessions. 'It's the same as when a woman has her menstrual period,' I said. 'She has to wear a pad.'

At once I knew I had misspoken; I was rude and undignified. Pa looked at me in disgust. Joyce-Ann stared down at the floor.

A day later Pa was bedridden and getting up to go to the bathroom was no longer an option. He didn't even have enough strength to hold the pee bottle. I called Home Care. 'How about absorbent sheets?' I said. 'I want no wet to touch his skin or bone. And the pulsating bed,' I added. 'The next step up from plain air. He's ready.'

On May the first, I brought over a pot of pink tulips and set them on Pa's dresser. I stood by his bedside. I hadn't heard him discuss money for days.

'It's unbelievable,' I said, looking at him. 'I've never seen cancer before. Never up close.'

'You couldn't know,' he said, and then he whispered, 'A new doctor came to see me. A big shot from New York. If I'll give him my kidney, he'll give me two kisses.'

'Will this operation help you?' I asked.

'Not me. But countless others.'

'Who is this doctor?'

'His identity must be kept secret. The surgical mask will hide his face.'

In the afternoon Doctor Kirshen made a note that Pa was having periods of episodic confusion. On a medical form that had been left on the kitchen table, the doctor changed Pa's condition from 'maintenance' to 'deteriorative. Three months'. Then he prescribed a stronger cough medicine and said Pa could take his puffers now whenever he wanted.

'Last night I saw my casket on TV,' Pa went on. 'I saw my shroud. I couldn't believe it. I saw my pallbearers.'

'Oh, Pa,' I said, 'really?'

'The grandsons carried the coffin across the Romanian Belts, not far from Kishinev. Goats were eating straw off the roofs. Not sheep. But goats. The ones with beards.' Pa touched his chin.

Joyce-Ann nodded.

'But she wouldn't close the coffin.'

'Who wouldn't close the coffin, Pa?' I asked. 'Who's she? An angel? Sheldon? Michael?'

'No,' he said irritably, shaking his head. 'They don't have the right.' He closed his eyes.

Joyce-Ann was standing at the foot of his bed. 'Did you have a dream, Pa? Did you have a vision? You didn't watch TV last night.'

'Not a dream,' Pa said. He shook his head ominously.

I pulled up a chair and sat down. I cried and kissed Pa's hand. Joyce-Ann came and stood behind me. She patted my shoulder.

'It's in the hands of the Lord,' Joyce-Ann said. 'Only the Lord knows the future. We don't make these decisions.'

'Don't cry,' Pa said to me.

'Pa was there when Davey was born, weren't you, Pa? He came to the hospital.'

But Pa didn't want to be steered into conversation. Talk gave him no joy. He didn't want to waste energy on remembering.

After a while, he said, 'I would have liked to save my brother.'

He was speaking about David. My Davey was named after this lost soul.

'Now, Pa,' Joyce-Ann said. 'Don't get upset.' She patted his leg.

'Maybe he was twelve at the time. He wanted to come with me. I left him home to care for my mother.'

'Oh, Pa,' I said. It was too painful. It hurt to listen. Maybe you'll see him soon, I thought. I didn't know. Who knew? I was too tired to figure out what I believed about the world-to-come.

'Look outside, Pa,' I said. 'See the green of spring. See the tree in spring one more time.' The window was open. The room filled with light.

He was barely able to open his eyes. But he could see the tree in full green leaf. The gauzy curtain billowed up from the floor, pink and flocked, cream-coloured and fleur-de-lis. Filled with warm breeze absolutely.

'You'd like to keep me here for a thousand years,' Pa said. 'I know you don't want to lose me. For everything there's a time.'

I began to cry again. I was kissing his hand. I was sobbing.

'Overwhelmed,' Pa whispered, 'overwhelmed.'

'Pa, look,' I said. 'Open your eyes.' The wind, the light, the greenness of spring, the *utter* greenness of spring. *The world is beautiful.*

The end was near. The end was coming. Sheldon was making soup for Pa in the kitchen, thawing chicken bones in the microwave.

'Pa's wearing a death mask,' he said.

'Don't say that,' I said. A gaunt face, yes. Brown, sunken eyes turning a filmy blue, yes. Bony arms outstretched in an El Greco pose of crucifixion, yes, yes. But a death mask? So soon? Already?

'What will happen to Joyce-Ann?' Harry wanted to know. 'Will she move on to the next dying person?'

I leaned over Pa to adjust his pillow. Pa shouted out, 'Are you trying to catch a word?'

I was taken aback. 'No, Pa.'

'What are the secrets?' Pa wanted to know.

'No secrets, Pa,' said Sheldon.

'Have you eaten today, Pa?' Michael asked.

'No.'

'He's giving up,' Michael said. 'He's refusing to eat.'

'It's not a matter of will. It's not a suicide,' I said. 'It's the disease process.'

'What do you have against Michael?' Pa bellowed out. 'What's between you and Michael?'

I saw Pa didn't trust me for anything.

'I'll watch the hockey game tonight with you,' Harry said. 'Daddy will carry you downstairs.'

'We could even rent a TV,' I said. 'And bring it up to the bedroom. It's the playoffs.'

'Can't you see I'm not interested?'

'You used to like the Maple Leafs,' Harry said. 'You were always a Maple Leaf fan. They made it past the first round. You should be happy.'

'I can't hear what you said,' Pa barked.

'Dontcha want to know who won the game?' Harry said. 'Dontcha want to know who played last night?'

Pa went to sleep. Later Harry watched the game by himself. 'From forty-seven feet out! Sundin scored. From a little pocket. What a shot! Sundin! Sundin!' Harry's voice echoed through the house, as if he were sending messages from the moon.

Michael convinced Sheldon to go with him to the funeral home and make arrangements.

'I never heard of such a thing,' I said. 'Pa is still alive. You should be at his bedside. Who knows? He may rally.'

'Call the ethicist,' said Sheldon moodily. 'Pre-planning is the wave of the future. We're meeting there at four this afternoon.'

At dinner Sheldon warned me that they'd acquired the memorial candle. Michael had placed it in Pa's bedroom. Then the children asked their father questions about embalming. They asked about the casket he and Uncle Michael had chosen for their Pa.

Later in the evening I saw the candle on Pa's nightstand. It was white and gargantuan, a candle for an army. I took it from the bedroom and put it in the living room on top of the piano. I covered it with a napkin.

Joyce-Ann said, 'We're not giving up. We have to struggle to the last.' Joyce-Ann tried to give Pa a dropper full of Sheldon's chicken soup.

'Swallow, Pa,' Joyce-Ann said. 'Swallow.' She tried to cajole. 'Pa loves his sons. Don't you, Pa? Look, Pa. Alice is here. Joyce-Ann is here. Wow, Pa. You've got a visitor. Wow, Pa, wow. You've got two visitors!'

Pa didn't care. His eyes were filmy. The chicken soup dribbled out the corner of his mouth and down his chin. I went to call the doctor.

I waited a long time for Dr Kirshen to return the page.

'I was over yesterday,' he said. 'Have there been a lot of changes?'

'Yesterday?' I said. 'Yesterday seems like a month ago. He's lost the swallowing reflex. His eyes are receding. And he's agitated. Very agitated.'

'I'll swing by. I'll have a look.'

'Thank you, doctor. Thank you.'

Dr Kirshen examined Pa briefly and then we went downstairs to the kitchen. He put a big brown weather-beaten medical bag on the table and brought out a pamphlet: *The Last Hours or Days of Life.*

'Have I discussed with you what to expect?' the doctor asked, pushing the pamphlet towards me. 'Did I give you this pamphlet?'

I shook my head and put one hand on the pamphlet as if I were taking an oath. I was crying. The doctor observed me with kindness and then made some scribbles on a prescription pad.

'His body is starting to shut down,' he said. 'He's getting ready to die. There's a build-up of toxins.'

The doctor spoke softly. He must've had lots of practice, I thought, trying to pay attention. I felt tears falling down my face. I licked salt off my lips. I was thinking of the doctor's first wife. Pa's going soon, I said to myself. My Pa, my Pa.

'I may put in a condom catheter,' the doctor said, thinking out loud. 'I'd like to put in the butterfly needle in case of pain. So far he isn't in pain.'

'How do you know? How do we know he's not in pain?'

'I don't see brow furrowing.' The doctor pointed to a spot above the bridge of his nose and between his eyebrows. 'This is where we see pain. Or in the scrunching of the forehead.' Then he went back to discussing the condom catheter and the butterfly needle for IV morphine. He seemed to be weighing his options. 'You can suspend with all the medications. He won't be able to take anything at this point.'

No more need for Zoloft, I thought. Give up on the antidepressants. Pa is beyond depression.

Dr Kirshen said, 'I'll write you out something for agitation that you can give him sublingually. And you'll have to read up in here on mouth care. Mouth care is very important.' He fished in his medical bag again and gave me one swabette. The swabette was a lollipop stick with a little cylindrically shaped pink sponge on the tip. 'You'll need to purchase more of these babies in the morning from a medical supplies store. You won't find them at the pharmacy.' He smiled.

I nodded.

The doctor sat for one more minute. He told me to go to the pharmacy and buy baking soda and fake tears and to get the prescription filled. 'It's not covered by insurance,' he said, 'but I think it's best to have this stuff on hand.'

When he left, I sat down at the kitchen table and began to go over the pamphlet. It was six pages long and full of information and directions on how to care for the dying at home. *We are aware that things have not been easy for you or your loved one to this point,* I read. *How long is not certain, but you and your family need to be prepared.* I went to check on Pa. He seemed to be sleeping lightly. *Always talk to your loved one as if he or she can hear everything. Hug, touch and cry – all of these things are important.*

I was not as lost in the pharmacy as I expected to be. I still had some presence of mind. I handed in the prescription for sublingual Lorazepam and went to the food aisle to get Joyce-Ann a bottle of Diet Pepsi. It took me a long time to find the box of baking soda, but I never gave up as my eyes roved along the shelves from crayons to fabric softeners to stationery. In the back of my mind the whole time was the image of Pa sucking on the eyedropper.

Goodbye, Ruby Tuesday. Who could hang a name on you? The song was piped into the pharmacy. Why couldn't I remember the name of the band? Why couldn't I think? I stood by the counter, reading the names on the little stapled white bags of medicines in a metal basket – Walter Eisen, Harriet Fructman, Jerry Pritchard, Naomi Glasgow. Were they dying, too? I asked the pharmacist in what aisle I could locate artificial tears. *Suddenly I just woke up to the Happening.* The Supremes, I thought, the Supremes.

Joyce-Ann was reading the pamphlet at the kitchen table when I got back to the house. Prudently she said, 'There's no more reason to give him the nutritional supplement.'

I called Sheldon to tell him what was going on; Harry was

sleeping, but Davey was up. Then I called Michael, 'Your father is dying,' I said.

'I know,' Michael said. 'I was there all day.'

'No. The doctor was just here. Pa's death is imminent.'

It was already ten-thirty. Michael and Barbara called their children. They came from all parts of the city. Within the hour they were assembled around Pa's bed. Barbara picked up the vial of Lorazepam from the dresser and examined it. 'I wouldn't give him this,' she said. 'It's too strong.'

I was wondering what kind of experience Barbara had with Lorazepam. But I said, 'Just look for brow furrowing.'

Pa picked at his sweatshirt. 'Oy, oy, oy,' he moaned. 'Oy, oy, oy.'

'Feeling any pain, Pa?' Melissa asked. She leaned over him and shook his shoulders a bit, trying to rouse him from his throes. Pa's eyebrows lifted and his hands twitched. He was startled awake for an instant. 'Oy, oy, oy.'

'"The person may be too weak to respond or may not be able to speak, but they will still be able to hear and understand what you say,"' Rory read. '"Avoid very loud noises."' He passed the pamphlet to his father like a hot potato.

Michael paged through it. 'Pa's got every one of the symptoms,' he said. 'This is some document.'

Holly turned to her mother and said, 'Jane Fonda got a divorce from Ted Turner today.'

'Really?' said Barbara. 'I used to do her workout. She's my age.'

Holly stuck out her tongue. It was pierced by a large black bead.

'Oy, oy, oy,' Pa moaned. He extended his arm towards his leg. This gesture took seconds, maybe a minute. Finally he touched it, as if to ask, *Is this a leg? Is this still a leg?*

A fungus thrush, thick and white, was already building up on Pa's tongue. In the kitchen, I made up the solution to cleanse Pa's mouth. With great care I measured out water, salt and baking soda into a Mason jar. I sat down by myself in the living room. I wanted to memorize everything – the paintings on the walls – snowy pines, clouds over mountains, boulders in a river. I took note of the furniture arrangement and the texture of the smoke-stained drapes. Fifteen minutes later Sheldon and Davey arrived. Davey stretched out on the bed next to Pa and held his hand.

'You've got to release him,' Michael said. 'Tell him it's all right to go.' I thought I could read Michael's mind. I looked at him with open hostility. Don't deny him a dropper full of liquid, I thought. Take the memorial candle out of the bedroom.

Pa's still with us, I thought. Thrashing, moaning, snoring with his mouth wide open, a hollow bruise.

Then Michael and Sheldon began to make plans for the night. Michael took over the bed next to Pa for himself. Sheldon went to sleep downstairs on the leather couch and Davey put a blanket on the living room sofa. Joyce-Ann went to her room. The rest of the group disbanded. On the way home I stopped at the all-night video store and took out a movie starring Jane Fonda. When I got in the house, I checked on Harry, got undressed, and curled up on the couch next to the dog who was lonely.

Halfway through *On Golden Pond*, the Jane Fonda character came right out and told Katharine Hepburn, who played her mother, how bitter she was about her childhood and about her relationship with her father. I found it poignant that Jane's own father, Henry, played him. 'Daddy always called me Fat Girl,' said Jane, whose character was now quite grown up and pretty. Hepburn told Jane that she'd always had a chip on her shoulder. Hepburn said, 'Bore ... bore ... bore. Life marches on. To go over the same sad territory again and again – your father calling you "fat".' Of course, I thought, sad territory often made a life what it was. I used to have a taste for the exploration of unhappy psychological regions. But now I was fed up. I wanted to let go.

Several people were in line in front of me at the medical supplies store. Hurry, I thought, I want to swab the mouth of the dying one more time. I bought a bag of fifty swabettes. By the time Harry and I got to Pa's house, mucus was bubbling in the back of his throat.

Davey was angry. He'd been stroking Pa's arm. 'Where were you?' he said. 'Pa's choking.'

'Didn't you read the pamphlet?' I answered with vehemence. I picked up the death brochure, opened to 'Gurgling in the Throat', and read, '"These secretions will never result in suffocation or death from a blocked airway."'

'His throat looks clogged to me,' said Sheldon.

'Now he's farther gone than Mr Guryadev,' said Harry, stopped in the doorway and looking at Pa. 'Mr Guryadev couldn't talk but he had his physical strength.'

'At least Mr Guryadev could eat,' Davey said. He was dismal and I was sorry I'd lost my patience. 'He could use the urinal and sip ice water through a straw.'

'The shower is to blame,' Sheldon said. A few days ago Pa had been too weak to get in and out of the bath. Sheldon had set Pa up on a plastic garden chair in the shower stall. '"Too hot. Too cold,"' said Sheldon, imitating Pa in the shower, blocking his head with his hands as if he were dodging blows.

'He preferred the bath,' I said unhappily.

'He loved his baths,' said Harry. He smirked when he saw his brother start to cry.

All day Michael talked. He sat in a chair under the window. The foot of his chair caught the curtain. It did not billow.

'I got a great deal on a painter,' he said. 'He'll do the house for twenty-one hundred and haul away two cartloads of trash. It's reasonable. He's got a kid in private school.'

'Can you watch what you're saying?' said Sheldon, his arm shooting up in a fascist salute. 'Do you mind not talking that way? Pa's soul is somewhere in this room.'

Michael said, 'I don't know about that.'

'He can understand every word,' said Sheldon. 'He hears everything. It says right here in the pamphlet.' He pointed to page two. 'Just read it. Didn't you read it?'

'We're going to take up all this carpet and find beautiful hardwood underneath.'

Pa opened his glazed eyes and took his arm away from Davey.

'What furniture do you think you'll want?' Michael asked.

'I don't know,' I said. 'I'm not thinking about it.' Everyone grieves in his own way, I thought. I tried to ignore Michael but he asked again.

He said, 'How about the TV? We have enough TVs.'

I shrugged. I held Pa's hand and stroked his fingers.

I recalled the doctor's advice on peer counselling. *Dear Peer*, I thought, *Don't you think it's too soon to divvy up the spoils?*

Sheldon took over sitting next to his father. He stroked his hand. 'You're surrounded by love, Pa. You're bathed in love. Do you feel the love around you?'

Sheldon passed me the pamphlet. *Silence often has great meaning when words do not do justice to the moment*, I read in *The Last Hours*. I wondered what clothes I had to wear to a funeral. Then I thought about taking in a foster child. I don't think I can take on another dog, I thought. And another cat was out of the question.

The death throes lasted three days. Pa was pretty much out of it. At first he sucked on the swabettes, but then he grew too tired. He didn't want his hand held any more. He didn't want to be stroked. His eyes seemed to be stuck shut. 'You can't really say he's hovering,' I said. 'He's making his way towards death. He's trudging along.'

I thought Sheldon was definitely feeling the strain. He had just smoked up in the backyard. 'Don't you believe in astral projection?' he said.

'I don't know,' I said. 'How would I know?'

'I read all of Carlos Castaneda when my mother died. Of course he was using drugs to travel beyond the body. I keep searching for Pa up there.' Sheldon looked at the ceiling.

I looked up and I looked down. In front of the bathroom was a light brown stain. The carpet had been difficult to clean. Wherever Pa was going, I thought, it was hard to get to. I hoped Sheldon wouldn't start talking about Hermann Hesse.

All day on Friday rain threatened. The sun never shone. Joyce-Ann went for a walk around one o'clock. Every few minutes someone had to swab Pa's tongue. His mouth was in bad shape, a tongue rubbed raw from swabbing. In the late afternoon Barbara asked Joyce-Ann to change his diaper. Joyce-Ann said, 'Pa, if I don't see you tomorrow, I'll see you on the other side.' After that Joyce-Ann had very little involvement. Mostly she stayed in her bedroom.

A cousin, called Cousin, came to the house and sat for a while. During the war Pa had rescued him from drowning in a lake. Cousin, a plump man in his sixties, sat at the foot of Pa's bed, weeping and wringing his hands in anguish. When he was ready to leave, he leaned over Pa, lifted him up, and squeezed him to his chest. Pa shook as if he'd been caught in an earthquake. 'Goodbye, Pa,' Cousin said in a loud voice, tears streaming down his face. 'Goodbye.'

'Pa's too far gone for passionate embraces and vigorous farewells,' Sheldon said when Cousin had gone.

'Why was Cousin shouting?' Harry said. 'He acted like Pa was deaf. Doesn't he know Pa has cancer?'

A still night, barely a breeze. The hum of the air bed commingled with Pa's moans. His face caved in on itself. At Pa's bedside the family kept up the vigil.

Sheldon talked about the war. Michael talked about the country club.

Barbara said truthfully, 'Pa has no quality of life.'

His breathing was shallow, raspy and laboured. But his brow remained unfurrowed. Howard sat quietly crying.

'"Remember when your loved one dies,"' read Rory. '"Do not panic. Do not call 911."'

Melissa manicured Pa's nails. Pa let her file and buff to her heart's content. Rebecca crawled around on the bed next to him. Together she and Melissa sang 'You Are My Sunshine'.

'He knows we're singing,' Melissa said gaily. 'He likes it. He knows we're here.'

The invalid's room was getting crowded. I was being squeezed out. I didn't even know where to stand. Pa's breathing became rapid. I didn't care that Pa was ready to leave this old world behind. I don't want him to go, I thought. I don't want to lose him.

Pa died on Saturday morning.

'Joyce-Ann and I were downstairs having a tea,' Sheldon said. 'And the bathroom door blew shut. A loud bang. That's when it must've happened.'

'Kiss him,' I said to Harry when we walked into the bedroom of the newly dead Pa. In that same second I remembered *The Three Faces of Eve*. What am I saying? I thought. Harry could end up with a split personality like Eve from kissing a dead person. Who am I to tell him how to encounter the dead? 'Harry, no. Don't. I mean I take that back. I mean do what you want. It's not up to me.' I looked at my son staring at Pa. 'Could you give me a hug, Harry? I think I need a hug.'

Harry hugged me.

'Are you sure he's dead?' I asked Sheldon. Gently Sheldon took Pa by the shoulders. He lifted him up a little from the pillow. 'Pa,' he called. 'Pa.'

But Pa was dead. He wouldn't answer and he wouldn't be moved. He had breathed his last. His mouth was hanging open. I arranged his blanket. I sat for a while petting him. I held his hand. I kissed him again and again on the forehead.

When Rory came, I said, 'Rory, I love you.' Rory looked surprised. He said, 'I love you too, Auntie Alice.'

Sheldon took Pa's hands and laid them across his chest in repose. Melissa also fussed over the body. She brushed Pa's hair, checked his fingernails, and tidied up his pyjama top. Then she wrenched two rings off his fingers, and Davey winced. 'Don't,' he said, 'don't.' Michael tried to close Pa's mouth, but his jaw was too slack. After a few tries, Michael saw it could not be done, so Pa's mouth dropped into its lopsided 'oh'.

Everyone took turns sitting next to Pa. I hoped Doctor Kirshen would be on call. But the answering service told me that he was away for the weekend. Then we had to wait a long time for another doctor from the palliative care centre to arrive and declare that Pa was dead, even though by now we knew it for ourselves.

The impression was that this doctor hadn't rushed over. She was carefully made up and fashionably dressed. High heels, a summer wool suit, and an asymmetrical haircut. Very haute couture for a house call, I thought. She sat down in a chair by Pa's bed.

'Was it a peaceful death?' she asked and began to write out the death certificate.

All along I had been giving blow-by-blow accounts of the death process to anyone who would listen. 'Not exactly,' I said, rather flustered. 'It was hard to die. It took a lot of time. A lot of energy.'

The doctor seemed not to like this answer. She was elegant and unemotional. 'He looks peaceful to me,' she said. 'Think how much energy it takes to be born.'

I wasn't in the mood to remember the pain of childbirth. *Dear Peer,* I thought, *she can say what she wants, she's no peer.* I started to cry again. I fell silent.

Finally the funeral parlour came to pick up the body. Two young men went upstairs and zipped Pa into a body bag. I watched them carry him down the stairs. Davey stood at the window. 'They're putting Pa in an Econo-van. With another corpse already in the trunk.'

'Person,' Barbara said. 'Do you mind saying person?'

'It's a business,' Michael said. 'They make millions. Figure three to five funerals a day. They stand to make thirty thousand every twenty-four hours.'

Barbara said, 'We should have a contents sale. Rory wants that lamp in the basement with the bulb that says B-A-R.'

'Why don't we just give everything to charity?' I said.

'Upstairs Pa cheaped out,' Michael said. 'He didn't put down an underpad.'

'I wouldn't worry about it,' said Sheldon. 'We're orphans now.'

In the Comfort Room the rabbi made inquiries. He was in a bit of a hurry, he said, because after the funeral, he was going to see *The Lion King.* Someone from the synagogue had given him third-row seats. He'd heard it was a terrific show.

'I liked Pa's latkes,' Davey said. 'Usually I don't eat latkes.'

'He made good chicken soup,' said Harry.

'I paid attention to his stories,' Holly said. 'No one understood how I could listen for so long.'

Sheldon said, 'Pa spoke seven languages. He crossed many borders during the war.'

'You're making him out to be a bright man,' said the rabbi. 'An intellectual?'

No one answered.

The rabbi said, 'A lot of history comes out in these rooms. My brother was in Alma-Ata. Then he went to China. And ended up in South Africa before coming to Canada in 1948. Quite a story he had. And what a memory for details. How about Pa? What made him tick? Tell me more.'

Dear Peer, I thought, *More what? With no hard feelings, tell the rabbi to shut up.*

Barbara whipped the shiva house together. She turned the dining table sideways and set it with platters of cold cuts, breads, salads and fruit. Folding chairs were arranged. The mirrors were frosted. I sat down on the sofa next to her mother, Claire. Some of Barbara's relatives were walking around the house holding wineglasses. There was a convivial ambience.

'He was always so negative,' Claire said. 'A bad word about everybody. And the smoke. He was a terrible driver, too. I never liked him.'

I said, 'I thought of Pa as my father.'

'You didn't do wrong, Alice. He was lucky to have you. But he couldn't return your love. He was too crude.'

I excused myself and went into the kitchen. I started to wash some dishes. The big window was open. It had turned into a beautiful day. Some people had gone to sit outside on the patio. Rebecca was jumping in and out of the pool.

The days of the shiva were long and tiresome. For a week I had to run back and forth between our house and Michael's, which were at opposite ends of the city.

'How come Barbara's not offering to send us home with food?' I asked Sheldon on the fourth morning. 'Not a cookie. Not a bread roll. Why does she get to stockpile? They wanted the shiva at their house. I thought people brought the food for all the mourners.'

'Why don't you ask her for a care package?'

'She should offer. Remember how Pa always filled a jar with chicken soup.'

'If you don't ask, you won't get.'

'I never asked Pa. He gave.'

'Well, Barbara's not Pa,' said Sheldon.

'She doesn't have a capacious heart.'

'At least not for us.' He bowed his head to his cereal. A signal he didn't want to talk further. I didn't want to press him into a series of hatreds. Maybe Barbara had used up all her generosity on her children, I thought.

After the shiva Barbara and Michael were ready to begin the job of dismantling Pa's house. 'Too soon,' I said. 'What's the big hurry?' *Dear Peer, as God is my witness, I'd say: Take it all. But I feel I have to protect Sheldon.* Soon Pa's house was in complete disarray. In the kitchen Barbara and I rummaged through stashes of unusable things, drawers full of shopping bags sticky with age, balls of rubber bands, elastics by the hundreds, plastic forks, soiled paper napkins, packets of Alka-Seltzer, shoelaces and keys. We threw away cans and empty greasy bottles. We got rid of Pa's two pocket knives (even though Harry wanted one) and cleared out the pantry shelves. Barbara divided spices and foodstuffs, while I collected twenty-six jars of freeze-dried coffee for the food bank.

We threw away his medicines, his false teeth and the bag of swabettes.

Then we spent one whole night going through old photographs. We sorted through boxes and albums. Michael searched for pictures of himself in the DP camp and turned up a Super 8mm film of his bar mitzvah. The photographs showed that after the war Pa regained his strength. But his wife had a crooked mouth. She did not smile in a single photograph.

After all, she had lost a sister and a baby.

'Pa had to buy penicillin for Michael on the black market,' Sheldon said. 'He almost died.'

Later the family had been happy. There was evidence of happiness. They had gone places, rented a cottage on the beach. Michael was the tall, skinny brother. Sheldon had a sweet face and curly blond hair.

Right away there were things Michael and Sheldon agreed on. Appraise the silver tea set, the living-room set, piano, chandeliers and the dining-room wall clock – call in somebody and see how much that stuff was worth, if anything. The dining-room set would go to Melissa, the samovar to Howard, a Viewmaster and cartoon discs to little Rebecca. Harry wanted Pa's old wallet and Davey found his passport. The object I treasured most was a sugar scooper with a wooden handle. It was a good one, old-fashioned with painted-red markings, and I had taken it out of the canister when no one was looking.

'Do you want this?' Michael held up a plastic key chain from the Grand Bahamas. We weren't being cheated outright.

'You should dig up the magnolia and take it to your cottage,' I offered. 'People do move trees for sentimental reasons.' Go on, I thought. Take a vase. Take a table. Take a chest of drawers.

A few nights later Michael began to unload the things from the china cabinet onto the dining-room table. Butane candles, wrapping paper, butter dishes, silverware, crystal, a ceramic sculpture from El Salvador. Then he started bringing out the Royal Albert.

'I always thought the china was nice,' Sheldon said. At home he'd expressed more than mild interest.

'This china set has got to be in the multi-hundreds,' said Michael.

I looked at the coral flowers on the inky blue and gold border. 'It's beautiful,' I said.

Barbara sighed heavily. 'We want the same stuff.'

'Set of twelve plates,' Michael said, moving fast and stacking. He directed his orders at Sheldon. 'See how many bowls are there. Set up the cups and see which ones leak water.'

Barbara turned to me. 'When would you use a set like this?'

I had trouble thinking. My heart was beating fast. 'For the High Holidays,' I said, almost whispering. 'For Friday nights. For company.' To eat off, for God's sake. What do you want it for?

'We never had a shower or a fancy wedding,' Sheldon said. 'We don't have a good set of china.'

'Do you know how much each place setting is worth?' asked Michael. He picked up a soup bowl by its handles. I shook my head dumbly. 'One hundred and seventy seven dollars for this bowl alone. A single place setting could be two or three hundred bucks.'

'The big serving tray isn't part of the set,' Barbara said. 'Neither are the sugar and creamer. The salt and pepper shakers are sold separately, too.' Then she added, 'Those things will need to be split up according to value.'

'Divide the plates six and six,' Michael said.

'Wouldn't you want a full set?' asked Sheldon.

'We'll order from England.'

Then Michael started bringing out the crystal.

'If you hear a little ping,' Barbara said, picking up a glass, 'it isn't worth anything. But if you hear a big ping like this,' and she pinged a wineglass in Michael's ear. 'This ping is real.'

'Which of these glasses are for red wine?' Michael asked.

I had no idea. 'Take whichever ones you want.' I paused. 'I was thinking you could take all this stuff and then we wouldn't pay you for the car.'

'I don't want to buy any of this,' Michael said. He pointed to fifteen glasses from a gas station.

'Do you mind if I take eight of those?' asked Barbara. 'I need them for the cottage.'

'Not at all,' I said. 'I don't mind.'

Then Barbara explained the coin toss. I pretended not to care when I lost. Barbara chose a trivet and I chose a set of steak knives. I was still thinking that I'd never use the steak knives when I lost a second time. My eye was on a painted fruit bowl that had been a gift to Sheldon's mother. I had hoped that Pa would make me a present of the bowl.

'I'll trade you the bowl for the porcelain figurines,' Barbara said.

'I'm not interested in the figurines.'

'I am,' Barbara said. 'I remember when their mother bought them. A lot have chips. So they're not worth much at auction.'

'At auction?'

I went upstairs. I threw myself on the deflated air mattress and started to cry. I sniffed Pa's pillows. Then I opened his closet. It was empty except for a humidifier.

'You got rid of his clothes already?' I yelled downstairs. 'Why? When?'

Barbara was standing at the door. 'The day the fluffer came,' she said. The fluffer was someone Barbara had hired to give her ideas on how to spiff up the place. 'She told us to start clearing everything out. So that we can make more money on the sale.'

'Let's not bargain any more,' I said wearily. 'I don't want to quibble.'

'Next time,' said Barbara, 'bring boxes.'

All in all we fell upon the house like vultures. We divided up sponges, bottles of bleach and liqueur, and gardening tools. More and more, I felt we were getting the shaft. Not that I needed Pa's sheets, linens or bath towels. I didn't. I was willing to take the facecloth that said HOMEWOOD SUITES. My grudge centred on Pa's car. Pa had said I could have the car. At the time I didn't care about the car, but things change. That was then and this was now.

Night fell slowly. The crescent moon was in the sky. Clouds were still visible, pressed against a deepening blue. I waited for Sheldon outside in the parking lot of the synagogue.

'You're still going to pay Michael for a car that has broken air conditioning?' I said. 'And that may need brake work. It's probably not worth the money.'

Sheldon was grieving for his father. At shul he'd been welcomed into the community of mourners. Each morning and evening he was going to say kaddish. 'What do we pray for in the morning?' he said. 'We pray that we are able to pray. That we are filled with gratitude for the light of day and the bird's song.'

'Michael has complete control over the administration of funds,' I went on. 'I thought you were supposed to be joint executors.'

'In the evening we praise God for the setting sun,' Sheldon added, 'I'm not worried about Michael. He promised he'd be honest.'

I was wearing Pa's grey wool V-neck sweater, the one piece of clothing I'd been able to salvage. 'I feel bad,' I said. 'I'm not secretly in despair. I am in despair. I hated the coin toss. I never won once.'

'You have to remember,' Sheldon said, 'they're not just million-aires. They're human beings, too. They ate off those china dishes, just like we did.'

When it came time for Rebecca's birthday party, I resented mak-ing potato salad for fifteen.

With detachment I watched the kids play in the pool. When Rebecca opened her presents, I walked away. After the cake, I started to clear the table. In the kitchen Michael was loading the dishwasher. Barbara was scooping the leftover potato salad into a plastic quart container.

I decided to speak. 'Pa wanted to give me the car,' I said. 'You knew it yourselves. It's not fair to charge us a penny.'

Barbara seemed genuinely surprised. 'You said you didn't want the car, Alice. We were going to buy it for Holly. We were going to pay you. Michael, isn't that what we discussed?'

Michael straightened up. He looked beyond me. 'I thought the matter was settled,' he said. 'Sheldon and I agreed on a price.'

I started to say that I had the right to change my mind. I wanted them to know that Pa's care had been all-consuming. I hadn't been thinking about cars.

Rory stopped at the sliding door. Rebecca was hoisted on his shoulders. They stood ten feet tall. 'You guys are disgusting,' he said, looking at his parents. 'We just sang "Happy Birthday". You should be ashamed.'

I agreed. I was ashamed. I was very ashamed. Rory hadn't included me in his denunciation. But he should have.

In the morning the rain woke me up. Pa is dead, I said to myself, there's no bringing him back. This is a fact of life. Why don't you face it? A shadow was stretched across the ceiling. I could make out an arm, a hand, a pointed index finger. What threshold is Pa crossing? I wondered. For a while I stared at the ceiling and watched the shadow dissipate into light. I turned over in bed and closed my eyes.

At breakfast Davey put a muffin on his plate. 'I liked Pa's coffin,' he said. 'You picked a good one, Dad. It was easier to say goodbye once I saw the body in the coffin. I knew he wasn't there.'

I took a sip of coffee. 'Where do you think Pa is? Do you think he's on the other side?'

'He's not here,' Sheldon said. 'He's not calling. I haven't heard from him. Have you?'

Harry couldn't find his shoes and threw another tantrum. He shouted at everybody. After he'd gone to school, I tossed the booklet *How to Explain Death to Children* into the recycling bin. Sheldon went off to meet Michael at his office.

In the afternoon Sheldon and I set out for Pa's house. A big SOLD sign sat on the front lawn. It was time to hand over the key.

The garage door was open. The last of Pa's tropical plants, the ones that hadn't found new homes, were buried under the rolled-up carpet. Inside the house was bare. Only a few glasses and cups were left in the cupboards. Every wall had been whitewashed. Upstairs, the bedroom curtains lay piled in a heap. Ice from the fridge was melting onto the kitchen floor. Inside the fridge were a rotten apple, a half a jar of horseradish, and the maple syrup that I had bought when I thought I'd be able to get him to eat a frozen waffle.

Was I the only one who wanted to hug the bare house? I wanted to cry out: Pa! Pa! Where are you, Pa? Don't move on. Come back.

A half bottle of Grecian Formula, Old Spice antiperspirant, a bottle of hydrogen peroxide, an aerosol spray for athlete's foot, yellowing cotton, one razor blade and an old toothbrush holder remained in the medicine cabinet. The white garden chair was still in the shower stall. Sheldon checked under the mattresses for money and valuables. But nothing was hidden.

We were through there. We'd picked the place clean. The back of the car was piled with plunder: books, records, cleaning supplies, a basket of tangled philodendron and an electric lawn mower.

Sheldon was standing at the front door, waiting to lock up.

But no, there was still more stuff to take – four rolls of toilet paper, bathroom deodorizer, two pocket calculators Pa got when he subscribed to *Time*. The plastic elephant bottle was on the kitchen table.

By the time we got into the car, the sky was starting to clear. Sheldon lit a joint. His voice was calm. 'This morning I gave Michael the money for the car. He said, "I don't need your six thousand dollars. I don't need one hundred thousand dollars."'

'But he took it,' I said. I thought, people do say things they don't mean. I said I didn't want the car. 'Oh, never mind. Let them lord it over us. We'll never win an argument. Barbara and Michael always have to be right. You could go round in circles forever. They won't change.'

'Yes,' he said. 'It's clear as day. Their position is written in stone.'

He took a long toke. 'By the way,' he said, 'Barbara took the silver tea set.'

'The tea set!' I said, filled with alarm. My voice careened right out of control. 'You mean the tea set is gone? But we agreed to sell it.'

'Michael says we didn't want it.'

'But they didn't want it either.'

'Michael says it's a memento. They already found a place for it in their dining room. It's theirs now.' Sheldon frowned and waited. He must have seen that I was shaking. 'Calm down, Alice. It's a tea set.' He took another toke and coughed. 'You didn't want it.'

I had to hold myself back from stamping my feet. I wanted to pound on the dashboard and shout out loud, 'Liars! Swindlers! Cheats! Thieves!'

'I'm bitter as salt,' I said.

He smiled. 'Fill the teapot. Pour the brine.'

I glowered at him for a moment. Then I opened the car door. 'I'm going to have a last look in the yard,' I said. 'I'll be right back.' The yard had been Pa's oasis. The word meadow came to mind. I slammed the door behind me.

'Take your time,' I heard him say. 'I'm not in a rush.'

The yard was a sea of weeds. The lawn a jungle of thigh-high grass. Mowing would be a problem.

I stood next to Pa's old kettle barbecue. It was rusty, dented, cracked. No one had made a grab for it. Both Pa's sons had new gas barbecues on their back porches. In warm weather Pa had used to cook hot dogs and steaks and hamburgers for us. Maybe I could take that barbecue as a memento, I thought. We used it more than the tea set.

For a few minutes I imagined Barbara's repentance. Later, when she came to her senses, she would say, 'How silly I was to sacrifice your friendship, your kindness, your high opinion of my name. For what? A silver tea set. *I'm sorry.*' But I knew that conversation was a fantasy and would never happen.

Against the fence, shoved askew, was the picnic table that had been left behind, nothing more than planks of rotted timber. At those picnics, where we'd all sat outside, Barbara helped get the food ready and she knew how to serve. She'd been beautiful and efficient. She wore long paisley skirts, and scarves and pendants like her mother. Sheldon and Michael talked business. I had tended the children.

I'd been bored, too. I was always thinking of the future. The promise of a better brighter time. With bold interesting people. *O! call back yesterday.* I took a deep breath. Then I bent down and pulled up a handful of long, dry, yellow grass.

Sheldon barely glanced up when I got in the car. I looked at the house. Pa would have been standing in the doorway. Or sitting on the front steps, smoking a cigarette. He would have waved goodbye and wished us luck. He would have watched us head down the street. But I didn't see him. He wasn't there. The porch was empty. And the magnolia tree had shed its final blossom.

Did I ever think the time would come when Pa would leave us to our own devices?

Sheldon backed out of the driveway and started to drive.

'I almost took the barbecue,' I said, after we'd gone a few blocks. 'As a memento.' I was clutching the dead grass.

Sheldon laughed. 'I think we have enough mementos. The house is full of stuff you have to put away.' Obviously he didn't want to wander in the ruins.

I was thinking about Pa. No one escaped his wrath. Even if you turned over backwards for him, he'd find a name to call you. In my head it was easy to hear him shouting, *Are you my son? You are not my son.*

'Pa didn't have an optimistic streak,' I said. 'He didn't bowl you over with hope. Or rest in inner luminosity.'

'He was my pillar,' said Sheldon. 'Now death is the great teacher. I don't want to drive down Hove Street again.'

I looked over my shoulder into the back seat. I wondered how we would ever be united amidst this debris. 'We got a lot of sponges and toilet paper,' I said. 'We've reaped well. If it's about reaping.'

'Not everything has a price tag.'

'Remember when I was pregnant with Davey,' I said. 'Pa said I acted as if I was the first woman to give birth in the world. He compared me to the women in his village. The women who never felt a wave of nausea. The women who worked in the fields until the labour pains started.'

'He could be uncouth,' said Sheldon. 'He had a peasant mentality. But he liked our kids best. Barbara and Michael resented him for it.'

I knew what Sheldon was talking about. Barbara had gazed at my swollen breast as if it were made of diamonds. Nursing was something she hadn't been able to do because her children were adopted. I was quiet while my memory polished itself up as quickly as I could say trivial tarnished silver tea set.

And thus I came to recollect how Barbara had helped Sheldon get the apartment ready for the baby's coming home. I hadn't known the least thing about making preparations for an infant. The spare room had been filled with dust, stacks of papers, drawings and piles of books. Barbara helped make that room spotless. Everything had been prepared. On a change table all the supplies were laid out: baby powder and baby oil and baby shampoo and baby wipes and a jar of Penaten. A bag of plastic diapers and twenty cloth ones with plastic-tipped childproof safety pins. There were little baby undershirts and flannel receiving blankets and a dozen infant sleepers that smelled like Ivory Flakes.

It hardly mattered to me where children came from as long as someone was there to take care of them. But I knew it had mattered to Pa.

'Pa thought blood was thicker than affection,' I said. 'That's a mistake. It's primitive. Your father was a barbarian.' I sighed. 'It's pitiful really. How I'm not the daughter. Not even a sister. And yet I keep all the facts straight. It makes me tired.' I sank back against the car seat.

Sheldon was turning onto the highway. He switched on the radio. Led Zeppelin. Jimmy Page. 'Whole Lotta Love.' He turned up the volume. 'What a guitar player!' he said, bobbing his head. 'Sounds great!' He was already rocking out.

I recognized the song, too, from my youth, which seemed a long time ago. I had no desire to even tap my foot. I watched Sheldon as if he were a stranger, someone I had never known before. He was wearing shorts. His legs were long and hairless.

He began to speed up. The road, like years, opened out in front of us. At home there were children to raise. We had values to impart.

'Roll down the windows,' I said, slightly aggravated. 'I don't want the kids to smell the smoke.' Then I put my hand out the window and felt the force of the wind. I loosened my fist, opening my fingers, one by one. Swiftly, instantly, the grass was swooped up. Scattered in unseen directions, borne away, possibly, to places not yet mapped. Pa is dead, I said to myself. This is a fact of life.

Too Much to Tell

Ella joined Group because she needed an occasional hug of mercy and encouragement. She arrived at the Women's Health Centre in downtown Toronto on an October evening and took the elevator up to the seventh floor. There she found the large, vapid conference room, sat down on one of six folding metal chairs set up in a circle, and resisted the impulse to hurl herself from the window. The only picture on the pale, pink walls was one she immediately detested. A Georgia O'Keeffe print of an open white flower struck her as lurid.

She'd spent the day doing a survey on mayonnaise with only a fraction of her mind able to concentrate on customer response. All day she'd been filling her head with expectations of this moment. In her baggy jeans and oversized T-shirt, which made her thin body look thinner, she knew she appeared harried and dishevelled to the women who sat, waiting. Ella was thirty-five years old. Maybe all she wanted was attention.

Ella looked around the room. At the head of the circle was Jean, the facilitator-therapist, a little woman with short-short hair and wide, empathetic eyes. Her entire body, except for her head and feet, was draped in a purple shawl. Matter-of-factly, Jean introduced herself and the others. The woman sitting across from Ella, Danielle, was tiny, dark and fierce like a fighting dog in skin-tight clothes. Next to Danielle was Sally Griffiths, who was pathetically overweight, and yet her hands, which she kept folded in her lap, were extraordinarily delicate. Joellen, on the other side of Jean, was a tall, elegantly dressed woman afflicted with tics. She wore velvet pants and an embroidered vest. Fifteen to twenty chains with silver charms dangled around her neck. Ella made out the Buddha, a dancer in an arabesque, a dolphin and harmony balls and felt sorry for Joellen's violent bodily spasms. To Ella's right was Penelope who cuddled a rag doll on her lap. When Ella met her gaze, Penelope's hands fluttered to her face, her ponytail, the front of her flowered dress.

Ella's veneration for these women was instant and deep. She felt a rush of gratitude for Group and slightly guilty towards Dr Lau, her psychiatrist, as if she were cheating on her. I'm normal here, Ella thought. I belong. Dr Lau would be jealous.

'You're just in time for check-in,' Jean said to Ella. 'Close your eyes if that feels safe. You all know why you're here. I'm going to ask you to sit with your hands open on your knees. Ready to receive. If you can, I want you to say, "Dear God, don't let me be bitter."'

Ella kept her eyes open. She suspected bitterness was the one thing these women all had in common. Jean said, 'Look around the room, Ella. We share in your pain. You're not alone.'

'Dad was fuckin' Mom with cucumbers and bananas,' Danielle said. 'And sometimes she'd get pissed off. She's still complainin'.'

'I'm sick,' Penelope said, patting her rag doll. 'But my brother thinks I'm irresistible. You could say we're romantically involved.'

'An infant was killed in the forest,' Joellen said. Her voice was low and rasping. 'No Name tied the baby to a tree and cut off his head with a sword. I carried the coffin.'

'You're the most marvellous bunch of women I've ever met,' said Sally Griffiths. 'My sister doesn't believe me. She has a house in Thornhill, a husband and a baby. She says, "Why don't you get on with your life? Instead of floundering in the past?" But none of you say that to me. We're true friends.' This was her welcoming speech for Ella. Tenderness filled her eyes. Then Sally started to cry. She buried her head in those delicate hands and wept. Jean moved her chair next to Sally's and put her arm around Sally's shoulder. 'We believe you,' Jean said.

Ella knew it was her turn. As each woman had spoken, Ella had been wondering anxiously if she should tell these strangers the truth about her circumstances. She'd had approximately five hundred and fifty-two sessions with Dr Lau over the course of six years. Reticence had never paid off with Dr Lau. Besides Dr Lau would never give her a hug.

Ella's heart was racing wildly. She was going a little blind. Surely these women were the last human beings on earth to abuse her.

'I was hurt,' she said. 'In a hotel room.' Group gazed at the floor. But Ella couldn't say more.

'Trust will move you forward, Ella,' Jean said. 'Right, girls? It won't take long.'

Everyone at Group had physical ailments. Sally was diabetic and able to vomit on command. Joellen had asthma. Danielle, stomach ulcers and sties. Penelope was full of strange and irritating pains. Candida affected her eyes, her ears, her sense of smell. She was afraid to get a Pap smear.

'The body doesn't lie,' said Jean. 'We use our bodies as containers for our feelings.'

Usually Ella didn't think of her tiredness as a physical symptom of distress, but now she felt called upon to mention her fatigue. 'On a daily basis,' she said, 'I'm almost too weak to get out of bed. Immobilized. I'm always remembering how I was locked into a hotel room with a group of men.'

'Have you seen a chiropractor?' Jean asked Ella. 'A kinesiologist? Do you know about radionics?'

Week after week on Tuesday nights Jean tirelessly explained. These five women were victims of failures in guardianship. They were in some ways worse off than the feral child who had been rescued from the wilderness and taught to speak, wear shoes, walk upright, drink from a bowl and use a spoon. People whose guardians had taken proper care of them could not say I Have Felt Like You. The women in Group had various names for what they were going through. They called it the abyss, the pit, the void and the big black hole. Sally, who spoke French fluently, called it *dans la cave*. She meant that at the end of the tunnel there was only the tunnel.

Outside of Group, they were all malfunctioning in their adult lives. Sally stole cat food. Penelope had lain down with a dog. Joellen was black and blue. Danielle was trying to stay sober and her seven-year-old daughter, Becky, was a difficult kid.

The rule in Group was that when one person spoke, no one else responded, offered advice, or passed judgment of any sort. No one spoke except when it was her turn.

'First, the appendix,' Penelope said. 'Then I'm going for a hysterectomy. I nearly hemorrhaged three times this morning.'

Danielle said, 'I met Deon at bingo. He's an Elvis impersonator. Becky likes him too 'cause he took us out for dinner and a movie.'

'My little girl was two years old when I gave her up for adoption,' Sally said. 'Love isn't enough.'

Danielle said, 'I'm leavin' Bob. Kept hammerin' away and callin' over to the neighbours how he wants some pussy and he's entitled. Told them they're better off with their German shepherd dog than he is with me.'

'No Name wants to take me over,' Joellen said. 'He wants me dead.'

'The dog's barkin' "woo-woo-woo",' said Danielle. 'Fuckin' drunk. Becky knows what's goin' on. What right's he got antagonizin' me?'

While the others were talking, Ella planned what she was going to say. The prospect of being able to say whatever she wanted always filled her with nervous exhilaration. She wondered if the women would be interested in what had happened to her in the hotel room.

'Market research is very boring,' Ella began. 'Even though it pays the rent.' Boredom sounded so trivial compared to the dramatic miseries of the others. 'I want to be a singer,' she decided to confess. 'But I haven't sung in years. My throat is always sore.'

'We're going to help each other,' Jean said. 'That's a promise. Before we break, I want you all to take a moment and pray for our sisters who are already dead or insane.'

When Ella next met Dr Lau, she was agog with excitement and the possibility of revenge.

'We do pieces of work,' Ella said sunnily. 'We say whatever we like. We're completely honest. No one interrupts us. I'm finally getting the help I need.'

Dr Lau listened in typical passivity. 'You sound satisfied,' she said. 'More than satisfied,' said Ella. 'I'm happy with Group.'

Pieces of work were not simple divertissements. Jean brought paper, coloured pencils and crayons. Ella made a charcoal drawing of a little girl facing a wall. Work with childhood photographs triggered even more reactions deep in the women's psyches, breaking through dead-rock numbness. The women recounted horrors. Accidents that weren't accidents, mock crucifixions, enemas, infections, abandon-ment, betrayals. They made up fantastical routes to escape from their persecutors. They wept and screamed; Group made a lot of noise.

Afterwards, Ella and Joellen would walk to their cars in the park-ing lot and stand talking endlessly in the dark about what had gone on at Group. Jean approved; she called such conversations 'processing'. They laughed and their analyses of pieces of work were astute and provocative. Sometimes they snickered, a bit too hysterically like teenagers in a clique. Mostly they complimented each other on their clever ability to survive. And then, finally, when it was very late, they would hug each other for mercy and encouragement and say good-bye.

Jean gave them gifts, handouts on how to take care of themselves. In her Group folder, Ella kept the Virginia Satir Growth Model, a page from Gallwey's *Inner Tennis*, a poem about the blossoming of a rose (Don't pull a seedling up by its roots!), and a copy of *Desiderata*. Ella and Joellen called the advice handouts the 'Come along, Ophelia' documents.

Group said affirmations every morning and night. (I am a good person. I do good things. My world is good. I am the river from which all life flows.)

'Can you take some time to compliment yourself?' Jean said. 'Can you take some time to brag?'

To help them exorcise their anger physically, Jean lugged in a tackle dummy from her home office. Ella put on boxing gloves and beat the dummy until her hands and arms were sore, and then she kicked it with her knees, legs and the sides of her feet until every bone and muscle was weary with revulsion. Jean called beating up the dummy 'healing'.

Jean strongly discouraged promiscuity, drug-taking and suicide attempts. She urged them to develop their talents and spirituality. Her list of symptoms alerted them to signs of inner peace. 'I want you all to grow up and do nice things,' Jean said. 'Like play the flute. Or take a trip to Costa Rica. Go ahead, girls. Do my bidding,' she added playfully. 'And watch out for frequent attacks of smiles.'

Soon Ella called these women her dearest friends. She would do anything for them. She wrote a résumé for Danielle's boyfriend, Deon, listing all his accreditations as Elvis. She lent Sally Griffiths a hundred bucks. 'I don't want your kitty to go hungry,' Ella said. She would stay on the telephone with Joellen for one, two, sometimes three hours a night when Joellen was frightened by some new flashback of satanic torture. Periodically she visited Penelope in the mental hospital.

'My mother's giving away my inheritance to the TV evangelists,' Penelope said.

Ella said, 'Pen, your mother's been dead twenty years.'

'They took me off Xanax. Now I'm on Prozac. And Buspar.'

'Maybe cold turkey's not a bad idea.'

'When I get out of here, I'm going to contribute to society.'

'Of course you will.'

Jean referred them to other helpers. Ella went to a body worker who had her squat before a mirror, to a Tibetan nun who had her throw rice into a bowl, to a hypnotist who smelled of burnt toast and to a homeopath who asked a lot of questions. Do you like to wear things around your neck? Are you afraid of rodents? Can you tolerate heat?

Winnie, the body worker, looked a lot like Liza Minnelli. She had a friendly cat that curled up in Ella's lap. 'Tabby can sense you've been hurt,' Winnie said. But the mirror work was really hard. 'Open the lips of your anus,' said Winnie. 'Let everything go.' How gross, Ella thought. But she ended up collapsing in front of the mirror, crying, and speaking non sequiturs for hours afterwards.

The Tibetan nun was old and interesting. She was called Chorpal Moon. Her mysticism was a combination of Zen, Kabbalah and Sufi technique. She lived on the pastoral premises of a Waldorf school. She told Ella how she'd escaped from Nazi Germany as Charlotte Goldman and somehow caught a ship to Bombay. There she'd studied the arts of meditation and aloneness. She explained how she had needed to humble her heart so that humiliation hurt her no more than honour gave her pleasure and satisfaction.

'Embrace adversity,' said the wizen-faced nun. 'Every hindrance is to be welcomed. One should not run away from anxiety and pain. Yoga can be used to quiet a restless, thought-ravaged mind. When I was your age, I did one hundred and eight back bends every morning.'

'Why one hundred and eight?' said Ella, who had a stiff neck.

'One hundred and eight names of God in Hindi. One hundred and eight delusions in Buddhism.'

'Oh.'

'Oneness is the only reality. Open your heart to the ecstasy of worship. Burst it open!'

'I'll try.' Then Chorpal Moon wrapped her in a yellow sheet, served her wild rice and green tea, and Ella felt like Siddhartha.

Dr Roy Leiden, the hypnotist, had a fine reputation in the city, but mostly for his work with men. He was a trained analyst, heavily inspired by Robert Bly, and known for inducing abreactions and curing 'the real crazies'. Placement spots in his weekend workshops and survivor retreats, which were held on his farm in the country, were highly sought after. Ella had called Dr Leiden's secretary many times before she was able to convince her that, even though she was female, she had serious childhood wounds from which to recover. Only then did Dr Leiden agree to meet her for twenty minutes in the fully renovated basement office of his grand home. In a small, darkened room, Dr Leiden, sat on a kind of tapestry step. He lit incense, played bongos, and asked Ella a lot of personal questions that made her feel bad about herself, for example, 'Why all this interest in your genitalia?' Ella, who sat in an opposite corner of the room with her head down, did not talk at all. Briefly she tried to follow the skeins of Dr Leiden's tangled poetics about her state of being. But in her mind all his allusions to nuclear reactors, rabbits' feet and the Underground Railroad did not cohere. Everything he said was punctuated by dramatic atonal thumping. When the session was over, he offered to lend Ella a video on anger management or one on multiple personality disorders, and the services of his wife, an expressive arts therapist, were also available.

'Her qualifications are excellent,' Dr Leiden said enthusiastically.

'Do you think I really need it? I'm already getting a lot of therapy.'

He thought Ella could benefit. 'Let her hold you,' he said. 'Or teach you to watercolour for as little as eighty-nine dollars a month!' But Ella declined.

The homeopath, too, had a beautiful house – pine furniture, Oriental carpets, a wood stove, batik fabric on the walls. She was in fine athletic shape. In her kitchen where she kept her mountain bike and pharmaceutical supplies, she mixed Ella an herbal remedy for injustice.

All these appointments cost Ella a lot of time and money. Eventually she narrowed down to Group and Dr Lau.

One cold night in December, about three months later, the phone rang at eleven o'clock. Ella recognized Joellen's voice. She had started to call Ella from phone booths. Joellen would swing her car over to the side of the road when she was feeling overwhelmed.

Joellen said, 'I need help putting myself to bed. Meet me at my house and don't bring your teddy bear. I'm allergic to the cat fur on it.'

'I don't have a cat,' Ella said.

'Well, something about him makes me sneeze. So travel alone.'

Holding Terror Bear, Joellen met her at the door and led her upstairs silently. Her husband sat on a loveseat watching TV. He ignored them completely.

In her bedroom, Joellen turned to Ella and said, 'You don't care about me.'

'Didn't I drop everything and rush right over?'

'You're trying to kill me.'

'Why would I want to kill you? You're my best friend.'

'Shhh, No Name will hear you. He tried to push me under the car two weeks ago. He's a murderer.'

Ella helped Joellen into the bathroom. She washed her face with a damp cloth, stood over her by the sink while she brushed her teeth, and helped her change into a nightie. She pulled back Joellen's blankets and sat down by her bedside.

After she was tucked in, Joellen said, 'I joined Group to make friends who were going to help me. But you don't care about me.'

Ella didn't bother to protest. She wanted to tell Joellen about the men in the hotel room when she was a little girl of five years old. But instead she picked up a paperback copy of *The Little Prince* that was on Joellen's nightstand. She started to read out loud: '"I was more isolated than a shipwrecked sailor on a raft in the middle of the ocean."'

'Oy gevalt, Mamushka,' Joellen swooned. 'Wallsy's hanging in the attic of the country house. They got Wallsy, too.'

Ella was irritated that Joellen wouldn't listen to the story. She didn't think Joellen even noticed when she left.

Dr Lau was wearing a peach-coloured suit. Her expression was as tranquil as a Vermont pond.

'Who's Wallsy?' Dr Lau asked.

'The warlord first cousin,' Ella said. 'I think the whole family was involved.'

'You've got your own troubles,' said Dr Lau.

'Joellen always travels with a pack of teddy bears. She's got a bear for every mood. Sad Bear. Disappointed Bear. Bear Aloof. Her bears wear suede boots and leather jackets. I have exactly one bear. One.'

'You should do more for yourself.'

'Watch out. Or you'll make me cry.' Ella stared at the Inuit sculpture of a seal on Dr Lau's side table. The doctor's last vacation had been to the Arctic. Ella took a tissue from the Kleenex box.

'Why did you go to Joellen's?'

'I've told you,' Ella went on. 'Joellen's an artist. A wonderful mind and she believes in angels. You know I admire her.'

'Can she help you to sing?'

'I led her upstairs by the elbow as if she were made of lace. Her crystal collection was laid out on the dresser. She showed me a rose quartz stone. You probably don't believe in the subtle energies from minerals.'

'What do you mean?'

'How energy can transform matter,' Ella said. 'You don't believe in anything you can't see or observe. Or prove in a laboratory test with rats and mice in a maze.'

'You sound angry.'

'Maybe I am.' Ella looked at her watch.

'We still have some time.'

'I called Joellen "baby" and "princess". She was high as a kite. Just rambling.'

Dr Lau nodded casually.

'When I walked home in the snow,' Ella continued, 'I thought about Joellen's childhood. She learned to ride a bicycle. Took ballet lessons. Her mother brushed her hair. I didn't have any of that.'

'How are you today?'

Ella paused. 'I had a sore throat in the morning.'

'I'm sorry to hear that. Maybe there's something you need to say.'

'Should I chastise myself for running to Joellen's beck and call when I have my own little inner self to take care of?'

'I think you need to build yourself up.'

'You're right. You're right.' Ella twisted the tissue in her hand. She made it into a ring around her thumb. 'I'm fine. You know, f-i-n-e. Fucked-up, insecure, neurotic and emotional. We say that in Group.' Ella paused again. 'I'm not a fountain,' she said. 'I'm not a fucking wellspring.'

Of course Group suffered setbacks. Sally Griffiths was caught shoplifting, and she spent a night in jail. Danielle got an AA medallion and bought herself a poke of cocaine worth five hundred dollars. Meanwhile, Joellen's arms and legs were full of bruises. Everyone assumed that that husband of hers got lively, but Joellen blamed No

Name and his conspiracy. Penelope was back in hospital. First, she'd had sex with her brother, and then she'd stabbed him with a knife.

Sometimes, comparing herself to the others, Ella considered that she was an everyday girl with everyday problems, but she knew that her thought of hanging herself in the bathroom and being found by people who cared was not entirely normal. Ella visited Penelope in the hospital, as if good deeds would help.

'Did you meet Eddie?' Penelope asked Ella.

'I saw him in the foyer,' Ella said. 'Playing the piano. I gave him his cigarettes like you asked me.'

'We're getting married. Eddie and I.'

Ella said, 'I noticed that he's blind.'

Penelope held her index finger to her temple like a gun. 'When his wife and kids left him.'

'Oh,' said Ella wearily. 'Are you seeing a shrink?'

'Yeah, Dr Erna Goldblum. Very classic shrink. She says Eddie's a father replacement figure.'

'I suppose she's right.'

'Who gives a shit what she says? Erna Goldblum, she's so uptight. I love Eddie and I'm marrying him.'

Back at Group Penelope wanted to know if anyone had seen *Baywatch*.

'How about Pamela Lee's stomach?' Penelope said. 'I love her stomach. The shape of her stomach is just very nice.' Then Penelope started banging her rag doll against the wall. 'I hate myself. I hate myself,' she cried.

'You mustn't hurt your doll,' Jean said.

Danielle said, 'I'm feelin' guilty. I twisted Becky's arm this mornin' cause she was runnin' 'round the house with a scissors. First she cut her bangs and they was all uneven. Then she cut the toothpaste tube. And green goop got all over my new blouse that Deon bought for me.'

'Hearing you talk about Becky reminds me of my little girl,' Sally Griffiths said sadly. 'My mother wouldn't believe me. My mother said, "Sally, get down on your hands and knees and pray. Ask Jesus to forgive you for doing such evil things." I stayed on the kitchen floor for twelve hours. She wouldn't let me get up. "You wicked, sinning child," she kept saying.'

Jean put out mats on the floor and spread pillows of different shapes and sizes around the conference room.

'Sally is going to do a piece of work,' Jean said. 'I'll lead you through this, Sally. You're already warmed up. Why don't we start on the floor?'

Sally nodded.

'What animal would you like to be, Sally?'

Sally groaned. 'A wolf,' she said. At once she dropped to her hands and knees.

'You can't hurt me,' Jean said. 'But you can crawl on the floor and bite the pillows.'

Sally bared her teeth. She crawled around on the mats. The flab of her stomach was exposed like the breast of a great white bird. 'Growl, growl, growl,' she said.

'Good,' said Jean.

'I had a little girl. She was two years old and her name was…. I can't say it.'

Jean's voice was firm. 'Say her name.'

'I can't tell,' Sally whimpered. 'No one would believe me. Not my mother. Not my sister. Not anyone.'

Jean pressed on. 'Secrecy ruins your life. Who made you pregnant, Sally?'

'My father,' Sally whispered. Then she added, 'Her name was Gracie. They changed her name to Jennifer.'

The others were waiting; they wanted their turns. Ella watched them compete for attention. Joellen was pacing the room with Terror Bear. That night he wore linen pyjamas and silver pince-nez. Penelope clutched her rag doll. Danielle held a crystal the size of an egg. Her shoulders were bare, tattooed and thrusting. An eagle swooped, the leopard lunged.

'I mean if Deon's askin' Becky for a blow job every mornin' before he leaves for work,' Danielle said, 'she's gonna start to act out.'

'No Name stole from me,' Joellen said. 'He plagiarized my soul. Everything I shared with him. Mantegna, the illuminated manuscripts, Giacometti. He took all for his own.'

'Viva Las Vegas!' Danielle said. 'Love me tender, my ass. I need a cigarette.'

'No Name can't stop me,' Joellen said. 'It's official now. I'm having lunch with Magritte. And buying his apple.'

'I hate my roommate,' Penelope said. 'She's a slob and she lies. Always breaks my things. And never comes forward.'

Sally gnawed on a pillow. Jean stroked Sally's hair. 'You're about to be born,' Jean told Sally.

Sally began to squirm her way along the mats.

'Push, push!' Jean yelled. 'Push!'

Then Jean blanketed Sally in her purple shawl. She spilt three drops of Rescue Remedy on Sally's panting tongue. She tried to cradle Sally in her arms.

'I want my little girl,' Sally said, looking up at Jean. Her voice was very soft. 'My little Gracie. She had a pink spot. Right on her forehead.'

Ella was tired of Group protocol. She picked up her purse and left.

When she got home, Ella turned the music up loud, stood in front of the hall mirror, and sang 'Heart of Glass'. The guy who lived in the apartment across the hall knocked on the door. Dave wore heavy glasses, a plain blue shirt, and jeans. Ella had seen him before at the mailboxes and found him attractive. They talked for a while and Ella learned that he was a graduate student in computer science. Ella didn't tell him to take off his shirt. She didn't say, Just keep your jeans on, for starters, and watch me, say, while I put on some makeup. Nothing romantic happened.

'He's a bit weird,' Ella told Dr Lau. 'We got to talking about movies. And I said I'd never seen *Ben Hur.* I thought he was going to have an apoplectic seizure. "You've never seen *Ben Hur,*" he spluttered. *"Ben*

Hur. Ben Hur.' He was actually spitting on me. Totally indignant. Ended up leaving in a huff puff.'

'Many people have quirks,' said Dr Lau.

'It's not so easy to get a bit of quiet affection,' Ella said. She paused, then added, 'I'm sick of grovelling. I hate Group.'

'You need a foundation. You need a daily regimen.'

'You don't want to hear any more. You've had enough of me.'

'Why don't you pretend to be normal? See what it's like.'

'Dorothy Parker let her dogs piss and shit in her rooms at the Volney Hotel,' Ella said defiantly.

'Okay, Ella. Time's up.'

Ella quit going to Group altogether. She stopped seeing Joellen completely. Then Dr Lau moved back to Hong Kong where her husband had an appointment in obstetrics. Ella was left without much of anything to fill in the time slots formerly occupied by therapy, and so, not long after she quit Group, she was glad to accept Sally Griffiths' invitation to dinner. Ella had thought that she and Sally could spend a pleasant evening together talking about how past family circumstances impinged on their present daily lives. When she got to Sally's apartment, the door was open a crack, but Sally didn't answer, even after Ella had repeatedly knocked and called out Sally's name. Finally Ella let herself in where she found Sally standing over the kitchen sink. Sally had already started in on a pail of take-out chicken. She was raptly licking brown, greasy stuff off her fine-boned fingers.

'Sally?' Ella said. 'Hi. I'm here.'

Sally's eyes were pale and desperate, not even faintly hospitable. Her skin was puffy and white and her grey sweat suit looked like it hadn't been washed in weeks. And there on her kitchen counter were fifty, maybe even a hundred, empty tins of cat food lined up like artifacts. The whole place smelled foul.

Ella inhaled the sickening stench. Then she said to herself, Get the hell outta here. Run for the hills. And don't look back. Save yourself.

She left Sally's apartment without saying goodbye.

In mid-April Ella was sick for a week. She caught a major cold with lots of mucus, stabbing pains in her chest and a fever. The fear of bronchitis never left her. When she felt better Ella sat down in her wicker armchair and closed her eyes. Unsummoned, a memory came to her. Not a fantasy. She actually remembered. She saw her father's clenched jaw and a group of men in the hotel room. They stood around her still, child's body. They were toeing her like the corpse of an animal.

'Is she alive?' said the moustache.

'She's in bad shape,' said the vest.

'What should we do?' said the bald one.

'Doctor,' said the pocketwatch to her father who liked to be called 'doctor' even though he was a salesman. 'She's dead.'

Then the child stood up. She grabbed the key from the hotel dresser, and ran to the door. She jammed the key into the lock, but the door wouldn't open. The men pressed against her back. They pulled her hair. She was too frightened to scream. No sound would come, and terrified, she swallowed the key. I locked myself in with them, Ella thought. Idiot child. *Dans la cave.* Trapped in there forever.

All these years Ella had been waiting to be saved. A wail of sirens, the shouts of men, thunderous knocking, and her father's obscenities as the police barged in and led him away. The truth was something different. Ella opened her eyes and got up from the wicker armchair. Her head was banging like cathedral bells. She couldn't escape them, but they couldn't escape her. Profound, fucking brilliant, Ella thought. *I swallowed the key!*

A year later, in the early morning, Jean called to tell her Sally Griffiths was dead. Ella was still asleep when the phone rang.

'I can't believe it,' Ella said. 'That's very bad news.'

'It took them three days to find her body,' Jean said. 'I think she choked on phlegm.'

'Poor Sally,' Ella said. 'Poor Sally Griffiths.'

They chatted briefly. According to Jean, everyone was busy. On the whole Group morale was high.

After she hung up the phone, Ella didn't quite know what to do with herself.

She sat down on the end of her bed. To mourn a little was only right. She cried a few tears. She picked up the phone, and then put it down again. She had thought about calling Dave, but he didn't know anyone in Group. Then she sat down in the wicker armchair and tried to read, but she couldn't concentrate. The letters danced in front of her eyes.

Ella knew if she didn't get out of the chair, if she didn't move in this minute, at this second, that she'd sit for the rest of the day. *Get up*, she importuned and she obeyed. She made her way to the window. This is what normal people do, she thought. They fill themselves up with activities. Ella looked outside. People bent to plant flowers, bowed to clean dog shit, strolled towards the subway.

Ella took a shower, got dressed, ate a bowl of cereal. She looked at herself in the mirror as she tied back her hair, spritzed perfume, applied lipstick. She began to hum 'My Favourite Things'. It was a song she remembered from childhood, sentimental and goofy, but it came to mind. Then she went for a walk.

Dear Natalie

Dear Natalie,

To say I don't miss you would be a lie. I knew you wouldn't want to see me when I came out of hospital. I heard the fall in your voice as soon as you answered the phone. When you said, 'Oh, it's you,' and struggled up for light conversation: 'Are you on your medication?' True, Dr Bergson warned me to leave you alone. He said it straight out. Patients like me and therapists like you shouldn't have anything to do with each other. You were busy preparing for an exhibition of your smudge paintings. I was reminded of all those great blotched canvases: *Stones and Pillows, Pianos and Manure, Castles and Hellholes, Butterfly Barrettes and Stigmata*. And your masterpiece in charcoal: *Eggs and Infinity*.

I thought you might like to know of my new circumstances. I have officially moved in with my sister. After Blake left, Susan needed me to help her with Mark while she was at work. Too much hubbub at the school and she finally withdrew him from the seventh grade. He was being teased by the other children. And even some of the teachers had reacted to him with vitriol and distaste. Each day I try to do a little homework with him so that he won't fall behind. He doesn't like the lessons I devise in mathematics or history; it's always unpleasant when he balks.

Everything has changed. After Susan and Blake first married she didn't want me around, especially after Mark was born. She said she couldn't deal with me and a new baby. And Blake certainly wasn't going to entertain his wife's deranged brother while holding an infant on his lap.

I moved in with Susan in the aftermath of your affair with Blake. Mark misses you, but that's all he says. He has no idea that one day his father walked into the house and saw you step from the bathtub before you'd even had time to reach for a towel.

Blake said, 'Natalie is wide at the hips.'

Bergson says I must learn to use my mind in healthier ways.

I remember Susan's hope when I first brought you to visit. She hoped that you could help Mark in the same way you were helping me. Now Susan says you are part of my *smrti*, a Sanskrit word, loosely translated as memory. Traces of you are left in my mind and will awaken new thoughts. Yes, my sister is becoming something of a Philosopher-Queen. In the mornings, before she goes to the library, she sits at the kitchen table with her cup of herbal tea and a paperback copy of the Bhagavad-Gita. She has given up reading the newspaper. Events in the Balkans depress her even more than she is already depressed.

With affection,

Carl

P.S. Surely there are enough eggs to go around. I would always be happy to share my eggs with you.

Natalie, how do you like this snowy day? I imagine that you are excited by the snow because it has been such a long time in coming. Now Toronto is covered in snow, glittering and sparkling, the newly fallen snow. The windowpanes are frozen. Icicles hang from the roof like daggers. The mayor has called out the army. Soldiers and tanks are making their way into our city. I was going to go downtown today to give blood, but they've closed Eglinton station. If you're listening at all to your radio, which I suppose you're not, you'll know there's a severe blood shortage.

Did you ever meet Arthur, Blake's squash partner? Maybe Blake introduced you. Broad and fit? A voice that's almost a falsetto. Years ago Blake and Arthur measured volcanic destruction on the Pacific rim. Now they've gone to a geology conference in Anchorage.

Have we sufficiently addressed Blake's homosexuality? Is Blake the only person you trust? I would hardly call him the most trustworthy of men. I hate to call him names – a manipulator and a sadist. He thinks he learned a great lesson in detachment when he went to teach the farmers in India how to grow rice on mountainous slopes. Ended up in Bombay or Delhi walking without his shoes, and saw a bloated cow floating in the Ganges.

'Don't disparage,' Bergson says. 'What good does disparagement do?'

The night before he left for Alaska, Blake arrived at nine-thirty when Susan had specifically asked him to come at seven. He wore a ski hat with a tremendous pompon. His cheeks were florid from the cold.

'Why doesn't Mark show you one of his magic tricks?' I said.

Mark sprang up from the sofa with the joy of something worthwhile to do. He ran to his room.

'What a strange, goofy kid,' Blake said. 'He's gaining weight. You let him watch too much TV.'

'Not so much. Today we studied soil erosion and Roman times.'

'He should be in school. Did you see the way he plopped himself down? You know I deplore fat.' Blake's eyes roved over me. He was thinking flaccid. I knew genetics were on his mind.

'My dime *likes* to play hiding games,' Mark said, smiling slyly, as he came down the stairs. He spread Susan's large red floral scarf, the one she got on her honeymoon in Kiev, onto the coffee table. He put a dime in the centre of the scarf and folded in the four corners.

'Hocus pocus. Poof.' With great ceremony Mark waved his arms over the coffee table. 'Will someone tell me if the coin is still inside?' He looked at his father, and Blake chuckled to himself. Mark lifted the scarf into the air. The dime was gone.

'How'd you do that?' Blake asked.

Mark licked his upper lip. 'It gave me the slip. That trick's called Hankie Pankie.'

'Hankie Pankie, huh?' said Blake. 'What's five times nine?'

'Your age. Six times eight is Mom. Uncle Carl is five times ten.' He stuck out his tongue. 'So there.'

'You make me feel old,' Blake said.

Susan veered into the living room like an airplane before it crashes. Her eyes were cold and blood-limned. It frightened me to see her face devoid of all gaiety.

'It's late now,' she said. 'Maybe your father will come on time when he gets back from his trip.'

As soon as he saw his mother, Mark began to work himself up. 'I float like a butterfly,' he said, 'and sting like a bee.' He began to dart around the living room, swinging his arms, throwing punches, narrowly missing his father's face, then banging him a good one on the shoulder.

'Okay, Mark,' Susan said. 'Let's go.'

Blake rubbed his arm. 'Got any extra straitjackets in the house?' At the door, he turned to me. 'Enough with the legerdemain. Have him run around the block.' He zipped up his jacket, put on his ski hat. The pompon had disappeared.

Tonight Mark and I ate alone. Mark said, 'Mom's on her way to becoming a vanishing expert, too.'

It would be nice to resume our correspondence. I await your reply.

Your old friend,

Carl

Natalie:

I can't keep pretending. It was Bergson's idea to write you. You put all your emotions into the writing, he said, whatever you're feeling, shame, guilt, humiliation, rage. You can put love in the letters, too. You keep it all ongoing in a journal that you keep by your bedside. It's a technique, he said. A therapeutic method, a tool. You don't mail the letters because that would be dangerous, even against the law. Gracious, no, don't show them. Not to anyone. We don't want to give Natalie any more ammunition against you. Just keep writing. When you've got all your feelings downloaded, sorted out, tamed and mastered, you can tear up the pages. You won't need them any more.

They will have served their purpose. Or burn them, he suggested, with a candle and a prayer and create for yourself a little ritual. And it's cheap, Bergson said. All you need is pen and paper. And you can do it yourself. Without me, ha, ha. No one's going to read it but you.

Spellers of the world: Untie!

Mark has no idea that an *ear* is in *hear*. Or that *here* is where you are. About *their* and *there*, he asks, What's the difference? The crisis in public education is inside my doorstep. I'm trying to help Susan as much as possible. This morning I changed the beds and cleaned the bathroom. The cleanser, however, was not quite right for the tiles around the bathtub. The white turned a mottled grey like the spots on an Appaloosa pony. As always the old fear came up. Remember how paranoid I got when Lady Diana died? And when they found O.J.'s bloody glove? I knew I was still sick and mustn't blame you for anything. Now I'm making my pasta sauce. I've just laid the fresh basil on top of the boiling tomatoes. Don't forget how much you used to like my spaghetti. The snow continues to fall. Mark likes to watch the bobcats. He likes to play in the snow.

Natalie, you do know that Blake is seeing Arthur.

Later ... Mark was busy all morning. First, he built a snow fort, and then he buried himself in snow. He didn't want to come in for lunch. But I kept calling him. Come in and I'll make you a hot lunch. A grilled cheese sandwich and a bowl of mushroom soup.

'Ugh,' he said in a loud voice, almost shrieking. 'I don't like that. I want ice cream.' He began to yell and throw big balls of ice at the house. I ignored him as any mother would. I went into the kitchen and started to prepare. Then he called from outside, his nose pressed up against the glass. He made the most horrifying faces.

In the afternoon the Chinese girl from down the block came to play. Her name is Minnie Wong. She has a cold, and her parents had kept her home from school. But when her mother went to work, Minnie snuck outside. She's a pretty girl, with fine bones, and long black bangs that hang in her eyes. Mark took her upstairs to show her his card and coin tricks. I was folding washcloths in the bathroom. And I overheard this conversation:

'Why aren't you coming to school?' Minnie said.

'Everybody hates my guts. My name's not Pudge.'

'You won't be able to catch up.'

'I don't care,' Mark said.

'You will if you flunk out. Can't get a job when you grow up.'

'I'll be a magician. Don't you think I do good tricks? I'm going to Las Vegas.'

'All they do there is gamble. Las Vegas is a bad place.'

'Who says so?'

'My parents,' Minnie said. 'They hate Las Vegas.'

'You listen to your parents?'

'Of course,' she said, sniffling. 'Don't you?'

'My parents met at Woodstock,' Mark said. Which was a lie.

'Did they?'

'Yeah, and then they went to Chernobyl. They know about disaster.' Which was true.

'How about your roots project?' Minnie said.

'On photosynthesis?'

'No. Genealogy. Ms Timmins wants to know where your parents and grandparents came from. It was due last Thursday. You're *so* far behind.'

'Never heard about it.'

'*Never* heard about it? *C'mon.*'

'Well, I don't care about it,' Mark said.

Minnie waited for something to say. 'Why do you wear one black shoe and one white shoe?'

'My mother lets me.'

'If you wore two shoes the same colour the kids wouldn't make fun of you.'

'They'd find something else. They'd make fun of my Uncle Carl.'

I kept stacking washcloths on the shelf above the toilet.

'What are you holding?' Minnie said.

'This?'

'Yeah, that pompon. Where'd you get it?'

'Want to see it disappear?'

'Sure,' she said.

I peeked into Mark's bedroom to give Minnie a smile. She sat on the edge of the bed with her legs crossed at the ankle.

'Look. First, it's in this hand. Then, this hand. Hocus pocus. Poof. Where is it?'

'Up your sleeve?'

'Go on. Check.'

'Not there.'

'That's the name of this game we call magic. Long gone.'

Minnie went home. Mark and I read a story about a levitating monkey.

Natalie, I send you my best wishes.

Icy streets, flying pedestrians. I went out to buy a bag of salt. On my way home I crafted a little strategy to avoid falling. I moored my feet, one at a time, into snow banks, all the while pretending that I was stepping into mounds of white, hot sand on a sunny Caribbean beach. Such an exercise calls upon my powers of imagination. Which Bergson says is good. The chittering grew louder and louder as I came up the block. Voracious, changeling birds. Uh-oh, uh-oh. What noise inside my head! Imagine my joy when I saw a hedge filled with a hundred small sparrows.

Just yesterday I was walking along Bloor with both hands full of shopping bags. I was loaded down with groceries and walked past a poor old beggar covered in rags. And I thought, One hand should always be free to reach into the pocket for the needy. Let my hands never be so full of packages that I cannot reach into my pocket. Let me never pass the harpist in the subway without giving him a little something.

This is what I told Dr Bergson about you. I met Natalie here at the hospital in an art therapy group. We sat at your feet like kindergartners. Meg Blitzer sucked on the hem of your skirt. Ratty Huddle stroked your shoes. Charmaine Wolfe braided the fringes of your long orange scarf. We got paint on our hands and you encouraged the smudge. Later, you took me to your favourite café. We had tea. You read my leaves. You discerned amazing things about me. Why would she do such a thing? said Dr Bergson. Isn't it unusual for a patient and therapist to socialize? She liked me, I said. She wasn't afraid. We went to her apartment in the Annex. At home she read me some Dante. She wore old velvet slippers and curled up in the chair by the window like a cat. I felt special, I said. I felt privileged. It was important to me. I took her to meet my sister, her husband, and Mark.

And then he repeated this question: Why was she taking a bath in your sister's house?

To wash off the paint. She'd been painting all morning.

Do you think this happened? Bergson wanted to know. Is this what you really believe?

It's a betrayal, he said. Sex with a patient.

I wasn't her patient. She was my teacher. Sometimes Bergson gets on my nerves.

Yesterday I smashed my toes into the wall while I was vacuuming. I don't think they're broken, but I have to squinch them up in order to walk.

When Susan came home I was ready to talk. I'd been watching TV. The subject matter was violent. Babies burning in Kosovo.

But Susan doesn't like political turmoil. So I said, 'Blake made all kinds of promises to Natalie. He said he was going to take her to Paris and buy her wonderful clothes. Dress her up and let her wander around the Louvre. Take her to the Musée d'Orsay and pay for a trip to Giverny. All this was fiction. All lies. And Natalie had never been so happy. Imagining herself in Paris on New Year's Eve.'

Ô douleur! Ô douleur! I'd like to bring you to your knees.

Susan shook her head. She wouldn't look at me. Finally, she said, 'Blake didn't make me happy. Especially when he looked middle-aged and yearning.'

I nodded and stretched out my legs. My toes hurt.

Susan never says a bad word about you. She doesn't mention your name.

Blake is back from Anchorage. The landscape made him ecstatic. He looks more robust than ever. Wants to talk about nothing but glaciation.

'We did Alaska,' Blake said. 'Arthur bought a diamond for his wife.'

We were all sitting in the living room. Mark was reading from his Houdini escape manual.

'"The public seeks drama,"' Mark said. '"Give them a hint of danger, perhaps a death, and you will have them packing in to see you."'

I said, 'People crave sensation.'

Mark smiled. 'Would you like to see me climb my way out of a mail sack?' He picked up the floor lamp and tried to hand it to Blake. 'Go on. Blind me with this spotlight.'

'What are you teaching him?' Blake said. 'I want you to know I don't approve.'

'Why don't you keep your horrible thoughts to yourself?' said Susan. 'What would you like him to be learning?'

'I dunno. Does he know the Kolosh Indians used to seclude their girls at the first sign of puberty? They hid them away in dark, filthy abodes. Only their mothers and female slaves were allowed to bring them food. The girls were forced to drink out of the wing-bone of a white eagle.'

'Oh, boy, that's interesting,' Mark said. He put down the lamp and switched on the TV. 'I want to watch my show.'

Susan got up and went out of the room.

I said, 'Don't make a hubbub, Blake.'

'Hubbub about what? You're letting the boy mangle his brain with popular culture. When I was his age I was interested in social justice. It was all I cared about.'

'Blake's trying to be funny,' Susan called from the kitchen.

'Really?' I said.

'Blake's jokes need to be identified. Then he's the greatest show on earth.'

I got up to get some schoolbooks. I wanted to show Blake how hard Mark and I were working.

'Whaddya limping for, Carl?' Blake said. 'Nazis been chasing you again?'

Natalie, my lines are open. I feel your presence everywhere.

At the subway the men were singing in Spanish, a beautiful love song. I'm thinking of you, Natalie. I emptied my pockets.

Wednesday, it was Blake's evening to visit.

'I have a famous trick,' Mark said. 'Let me show you.'

Blake and I sat down on the sofa. Mark stood in the centre of the living room. He stretched out one arm and bent it at the elbow. Then in his other hand he produced a knitting needle. Slowly he began to insert the needle into the fold of his bent arm.

'Do I look like I'm hurting myself?' Mark asked. He groaned, swayed and knotted up his face. Some blood began to trickle out the side of his mouth.

'I must be a glutton for punishment,' Blake said. 'Why do I keep coming back here?'

'Don't you like this trick?' Mark clutched his arm, his stomach, neck and knees. More blood appeared. Blood dripped on his pants and T-shirt, and onto the carpet.

'You'd better clean this rug before your mother gets home,' Blake said.

And mottle it. No thank you.

Mark moaned some more, fell to the floor, rolled in blood.

'Your mother's going to have a fit,' said Blake.

I said, 'I'll clean up.'

Blake said, 'Mark, you'd better go wash.' He looked at his watch. 'She's going to blame me for this little episode.'

'Aren't you going to clap?' said Mark. 'I'm really hurting.'

'I can tell,' Blake said.

'Where's the applause? Where's the applause, Daddy-o?' Mark stomped upstairs and pillaged in his bedroom. He slammed some drawers open and shut. Complained when he turned on the bath water. We heard him in Susan's room. For some time we listened to his rumpus.

'Been to any good restaurants lately?' Blake said.

'Naw, I don't get out much. Hardly at all.'

'You'll go crazy if you stay cooped up here.'

'Thank you, Blake. What a friendly thing to say.'

We sat for a while in quiet until Blake leapt up.

We found Mark face down in the bathtub. He was in his boxers. His hands were handcuffed behind his back and his feet were tied with the belt of Blake's old bathrobe. I turned off the water.

'Help me get him out of the tub,' Blake said. 'He must've banged his head. Why'd you buy him these handcuffs?'

'They aren't real handcuffs.'

We pulled Mark from the tub and laid him out.

I just stood there looking at Mark. He seemed to ooze onto the bathroom floor. *Go on. Just lay your blubber down.*

'Carl, snap out of it. Call 911. And find the key to these cuffs.'

Blake was kneeling and breathing into Mark, compressing his chest. 'Is there a pulse?' I yelled. 'Does he have a pulse?' The key was on the pile of folded washcloths. I freed his hands and untied his feet. I brought in quilts from the bedroom. When the paramedics arrived, they thought we'd murdered him. Then they realized the blood wasn't real. Fake blood was smeared on everything. And the sunset was strong, glaring in through the window, turning the light red, pink, and orange upon the tiles.

Natalie, what are you waiting for? For God's sake, get in touch.

To houdinize is to escape. Check out your Funk and Wagnalls circa 1930.

Yesterday was wasted. Stayed home and fell asleep while willing a change in consciousness. I dreamt about the people from the hospital. Ratty Huddle was gnawing at my stomach. Charmaine Wolfe was taking off her nightgown. And Meg Blitzer was doing her impression of Blanche Dubois. Very entertaining stuff. Woke up with a million more things to think about.

Today was better. I was able to trick myself for a while. I imagined that we brought Mark home from the pediatric ward. And that later we would do something special to celebrate. Then I had my appointment with Dr Bergson. He seemed more nervous than usual, blinking rapidly.

I said, 'I'd like to be cured as quickly as possible. I can't take any more hubbubs.'

'Keep it simple, old fella,' he said. 'One step at a time. It takes courage to admit Mark is dead.'

At the gravesite, there was snow in Susan's eyes. She kept rubbing her eyes. The cemetery people were trying to keep the hole in the ground from filling up with snow. It was impossible. After the funeral, the Wongs, who hate Las Vegas, came back to the house with Arthur and Arthur's wife, Lois. The coroner didn't insist on an autopsy. Mark cracked his head on the faucet and he drowned.

'Maybe he thought he could float,' said Mrs Wong. She wore her long black hair wrapped in a bun. She looked very sad sitting on the couch next to Susan and holding her hand.

'No,' Minnie said. 'He was trying to create the Chinese Water Torture Cell. Houdini's last stunt. He told me.'

'When did you see Mark?' said Susan.

Mrs Wong shook her head.

Susan began to cry. 'I didn't believe Mark when he told me Minnie came over. I said, "Do you think you can pull a friend out of a hat like a rabbit?"'

'My, my,' Mrs Wong said. She patted Susan on the back. 'There, there.'

Blake and Arthur were talking to Mr Wong about Alaska. 'Some Indian tribes still bury the bones of beavers,' Arthur said with sonority. 'To insure a plentiful hunt.'

'Why?' Mr Wong asked.

'So the dogs won't get at them and chew them up,' said Blake. 'It's a sign of respect.'

Again, I told Bergson I want to go away.

'Why?' he asked. 'Are you feeling responsible for Yugoslavia?'

'No,' I said. 'There are too many gravesites. Too many refugees. It's not my fault when a whole nation disappears.'

'Good,' he said. 'Improvement.'

Susan came out of her bedroom at four. She looked terrible, absurd, her face splotched from crying. I tried to give her some food, a cup of lemon zinger, a slice of buttered toast. Read her this from the Gita:

> Even murderers and rapists,
> tyrants, the most cruel fanatics,
> ultimately know redemption
> through my love, if they surrender
>
> to my harsh but healing graces,
> Passing through excruciating
> transformations, they find freedom
> and their hearts find peace within them.
>
> I am always with all beings;
> I abandon no one. And
> however great your inner darkness,
> you are never separate from me.
>
> Let your thoughts flow past you, calmly;
> keep me near, at every moment;
> trust me with your life, because I
> am you. More than you yourself are.

'Bullshit,' Susan said. I don't think she likes me.

'Nonsense,' said Bergson. 'Don't be silly, Carl. She needs you. Your life has meaning.'

Maybe he's right. Who knows, Natalie, who knows? Even though I'm clumsy, I'm big. I'm strong. I know how to smudge. I'd like to hand out cereal boxes to people who've been terrorized.

Stop, stop. What is it? What do you hear, Uncle Carl? Everywhere, everywhere, the sad song of melting snow, overflowing the gutters.

Mark's trick with the pompon was simple. Let me tell you how it's done. You look like you're grabbing it, but it's already stuffed deep in your pocket. All you are grabbing is air. Really there's no magic at all.

Listen, Natalie, it's probably best if you leave me alone. Don't come, whatever you do. Just stay out of my way.

How will I remember you, dear Natalie? Of course I always will. Long after these pages are on fire and the words have turned to ash. The smell of smoke remains.

The Middle of the Triangle

Joel

I'd been moping around the apartment all that morning feeling sorry for myself. I wasn't doing Phyllis Diller's hair. After Blair's funeral a bunch of us had gone dancing at the Barn, and I'd already told a dozen people that I'd be on Phyllis Diller's television crew.

Then my brother, Robert, called to tell me that Edward was in a coma. What I didn't need was more bad news.

I'm going to ride this one like a wave, I said to myself. Oooh, baby, I'm a surfer.

For the record, I didn't say to Robert, Oh, I'm not surprised. I heard that Edward had been acting up lately. And I didn't say, I heard he was drinking too much. Acting loud and obnoxious and getting into situations. Even if I had, I could be excused. Everyone had gossip about Edward's bad-boy behaviour and about his drinking. But getting his head kicked in was extreme, even for Edward.

I was still angry with Robert because of his affair with Karen. I could hear it in my voice. I was tired of his cheating on his wife with my friends. He must've broken her heart. I didn't have details, only now I didn't have a place to stay in New York. The last time I was in Manhattan, Karen wouldn't even speak to me on the phone. I had taken her picture down from the fridge.

'Blair died on Saturday,' I said. 'We buried him yesterday. Louie's in the Bell Wing with pneumonia. I've got to take Peter for his chemo tomorrow. He's got KS all over his legs.' Then I was full of questions. 'What hospital is Edward at? How long will it take you to get to Toronto? Where should we meet?'

'I can't believe Blair is dead,' said Robert.

'Well, he is. The last time we saw Patty Labelle he was wearing his Versace jeans. He got up on the stage when she was singing "I Can't

Complain". She gave him a great big hug. He was stoned out his mind. Wild. Just wild. That was less than a year ago. I can't believe it myself. He was such fun.'

I hung up the phone and the doorbell rang. Jane, my ten o'clock, was in the hallway, pulling a long face.

'Well, well,' I said, as I let her into the apartment. 'Are we doing Jane's hair today? Are you here for a little B and T? Bang and trim? How was your weekend, lovie? Tell me all about it. Can't wait. Come on in.'

Janie sat down and I pulled alongside her on the swivel stool. I began to brush out her hair. I knew what she wanted. 'Let's misbehave and mystify, Janie dear,' I said. 'Let's talk about misdemeanours and misd'amours. Play misty for me, dah-ling. Spritz. Spritz.'

I got out the comb and the clips.

'Philip's been wearing that little bikini around town that lets the sun's rays in,' I said. 'Driving around in a convertible like an Egyptian god. He's totally from the seventies. I suppose it wasn't meant to be.'

'But, Joel, Philip's the first lover who really respected you,' Jane said.

'And a liar too. Now don't get me started or I won't be able to concentrate. He's someone, excuse my French, who would fuck you over, then laugh in your face. Take his new boy toy for a ride in your car. Walk in the dog-piss park and then stick his gym shoes up on your sofa.'

'Oh,' said Jane. 'So he's not for you.'

I watched her lightening up.

'Breathe, Janie. You're huffing. Take a look in the mirror. One-half Jane. One-half Cousin It. Have I taught you how to cleanse your aura with sea salt and water?'

She shook her head vigorously.

But I hadn't the heart to go on. I was thinking about Edward, lying in the General with his head caved in.

'You know, Jane,' I said. 'On second thought, I'd better just stick to the snips.'

Jane

Joel's friends are dropping like flies. I met Blair last year at Joel's birthday party. He said he liked my shoes, my thooes, he said. He'd already had encephalitis and pulled through with minor dementia. I could hardly tell because I didn't know him before. But it affected his speech. He's dead now.

Edward Whitby's death was very intriguing to me. Because Joel and his brother, Robert, are very discreet, I tried to hold my fascination in check. And my will to do good. After all, Edward Whitby was a doctor.

The police caught Billy Junior Billet in less than a week. He'd used Edward's credit cards to buy groceries and stay in motels. Even before he assaulted Edward, Billy stood accused of issuing death threats and possession of a dangerous weapon. He would have lots of court appearances and that's where I planned to do my work.

At the time I thought, I'm going to see this one through. I'm going to go to the courtroom and take notes. I'm going to get down to City Hall every morning. I'm going to be a regular reporter writing about crime.

'Don't fall in love with my brother,' Joel said.

I assured him, 'That's not what this is about.'

Robert astonished me when I met him. First, the absolute Marlboro Man size of him, vast, tall, muscular. He began to size me up immediately in an almost primitive way. Me, Man. You, Woman. I got the feeling I was being evaluated like livestock. We were in a little café called Sweet Encounters, not far from Edward's apartment, where Robert was sorting things out. We ate off plates with pictures of dark fruit.

'I brought in my thesis proposal on John Keats,' I said, placing the document on the table in front of him. 'Just see if you like my style.'

Then he shot back a whisky. I saw he had no inclination to read.

'I want to fight for justice,' I went on. 'In fact, I just finished Primo Levi's *Survival in Auschwitz*. I try to read it once a year. We cannot wait for the lumpenproletariat to revolt!'

Robert looked at me the way the Spanish peasants greeted Napoleon in Goya's *The Third of May*.

'My people wore the yellow star,' I said. 'You know about the pink triangle?' He nodded, as if he thought I'd already judged him to be a good-looking man without a brain in his head.

I tried to explain. 'I want to protest against senseless death,' I said. 'I'll interview you and Joel and everyone who was in the club that night. I'm not afraid to meet new people. I might talk to Billy. I've a list of questions I'm already formulating. I can be quite dogged and persevering when I've made up my mind. For example, how did your parents treat you, Billy? Did they put you in any organized sports? Can I call you Junior, Billy? Did you learn to ride a bicycle? Were you on your own an inordinate amount of time? Were you exposed to music? Did you feel neglected? Were you abused? Is the world for you a misery?'

'Edward's family is conservative,' said Robert. 'They want to lay his death to rest.'

'A gay-bashing?' I said. 'A doctor's murder? The world needs to know what happened to Edward Whitby. To forget is wrong. Dead wrong.'

'We may be remiss,' said Robert. He paused to look at me. 'Did my brother do that to your hair?'

Robert

The call came in the middle of the night. I was dreaming about Denise and her freckles. My wife, Sandra, handed me the phone. It was Edward's sister. She was flying in from California.

Sandra was very concerned about Edward. We'd all been friends in high school. She helped me to pack. She walked me to the car. 'Be careful driving,' Sandra said. 'I'll hold the fort. Children, kiss your father goodbye.'

I knew Edward wasn't going to make it as soon as I saw him. He never came to. He never squeezed my hand. He had massive brain injuries.

Joel came to the hospital and we waited eight days for Edward to die. The nurses called it 'lingering'. Joel told me he had AIDS. He said, 'I've done the Louise L. Hay *From Pain to Power* workbook. I've done the Susan Jeffers' *Feel the Fear and Do It Anyway* workshop. I've taken the *Course in Miracles*. I've been speaking to a counsellor at Mount Sinai for two years. I want to make you executor of my living will.'

Sharon Whitby-Rose, Edward's sister, arrived from the airport. She reminded me of a horse, clipping along at a trot, as she dealt with the hospital staff and the funeral home. She was polite, but she needed to return to her family and work. On the day the life support machines were disconnected, we had a drink in the lobby of her hotel. She'd aged. Her blond hair was greying, but I insisted she looked exactly the same as when I'd seen her last. She took photographs out of her wallet and showed me a picture of her daughters. She asked me if I minded looking after Edward's apartment.

'It's the least I can do under the circumstances,' I said. It was nothing. I would stay in Toronto. I would stay with Denise.

Denise said, 'You don't really love me.'

And I said, 'Honey, I want to love you on the ceiling of the White House.'

Then Joel met Denise. At first, he was shocked that I brought her along, but he liked her. Denise is foxy. Very foxy. They became acquainted.

Joel sang a few bars of 'Sonny Boy' in his high, creaky voice. '"Friends may forsake me, O, let them forsake me".'

And I gave Joel a lot of Edward's stuff – his toaster, his blender, some towels and books. Edward's houseboy, Phan, had already made off with more than his fair share. Cleared out with clothes, CDs, spare change, and jewellery. He was that quick.

Then there was Jane, the graduate student. One of my brother's clients. She wanted to write something about Edward's death – a documentary or a radio play, just about anything. Maybe it was a mistake that I agreed to meet her in the first place. She wanted to get my voice on tape.

I knew Sandra wouldn't mind my meeting with Jane, because Jane had dark hair on her upper lip and a very nervous manner. But if Sandra found out about Denise, I'd be strung up as soon as the rooster crows come dawn.

Metaphorically speaking, huh, Jane. You're the thesis writer.

I told Jane I was going to have one more drink. Did she want another glass of water?

Joel

When we were at Edward's apartment, Robert slapped my back and said, 'You've always come through for me, little brother. Don't get Pollyanna on me about Denise.'

'Denise,' I said. 'Oh, Denise. I'm certainly not going to be the pot calling the kettle black, now am I?' Denise, I thought. She's pretty, petite, nice haircut, little heart-shaped silver earrings. 'She'll want to marry you,' I said.

I looked out the window. I saw activity on Church Street, down on Gerrard. I knew what was happening on Yonge. In my mind I could follow the route Edward took from his apartment to his office to his club. Geometric certainty until he got knocked off the predictable plane.

I'd lost so much hair. I was thinking it was the medication and I'd have to go back to the dermatologist. But each night I was praying for my hair. I didn't want to talk to anybody about my health.

Jane wanted to know everything. The names of the medications, their effects, the schedule of ingestion. She asked if Edward had been my doctor.

She wanted to know about sex. 'Is it safe?' she said. Oh, she was so responsible, but I wondered if she fucked. 'What about the commingling of fluids?' she asked.

'What kind of sex are you talking about? Down and dirty? Or virtuous?' I said, and gave up. 'Just leave the semen lying in a pile.'

Mom wanted to know why I hadn't told her about *the* AIDS.

'I was always hoping you'd change,' she said. 'You had a defective relationship with your father. He was always cold and withdrawn. Holding you at bay like a little bag of doggy doo.'

When I was sixteen, Dad found me with a boy, necking in the living room. 'Animals do that,' he said. 'That's how cows behave in the barn. But you have a mind, Joel. Pick the right way to live.'

I said, 'Mom, you're still talking about you and Dad. I've been dressing up like Judy Garland since I was eleven. Look around this apartment. My whole place is a shrine to *The Wizard of Oz.*'

'Who do you think gave you this disease?' Mom said. 'Where do you think you got this from? If you're sick, Joel, you'll need more than friends dropping by with a pot of soup. You'll need someone to scrub the floor. Wash the toilet. You won't want to leave anything open for opportune infection. After a few days everything is covered in dust. Are you on *narcotics?*'

Mommy Dearest. Mommy Psychobabble. Mommy blah blah blah blah.

'Did Edward Whitby have a diary?' Jane wanted to know.

His whole apartment was a diary.

I told her the community didn't rally. Some people thought Edward had it coming to him.

'He was a bad boy with a big mouth,' I said. 'The turtles and ostriches just tucked in their heads.'

'Can you explain that to me again?' said Jane. 'The community's position?'

Talk about attention deficit disorder. I couldn't concentrate on a thing she said. I was thinking about that last night at the Barn when I was a magnet. All evening I'd had the pretty witches following me around playing peekaboo.

Then Philip had come over with his handsome kindergartners. Philip, fresh from his appointment at the Addiction Research Foundation, carting his placebos, ready for the next instalment of chills and spills. Why all that riff-raff? I thought. Why those silver nails? And he accused me of being paranoid.

Jane's eyes flickered with confusion.

'Do you mind if we call it quits here, Janie?' And I motioned for her to turn off the tape. 'I'm tired,' I said. 'I feel like an old lady. Yesterday, I slept all day. Hey, I am an old lady.'

Jane

Already a lot of emotion associated with this play. I love the intensity. I'm going to call it *The Middle of the Triangle* in honour of the place where Edward was killed.

Billy Billet, out on bail, sitting in a bar, had no remorse. His eyes were hard and mean. Billy Billet thought he was above them all, the shitty queers.

'I would castrate every one of them,' he said. 'I don't give a shit.'

Why is there not a human dust hole into which to tumble such fellows? wrote Keats of a local tyranny.

I said, 'Was Edward Whitby attracted to you?' Could it be Billy was repressed?

'Edward Whitby told me to shut the fuck up,' said Billy. '"I've had it with you, Billy," he said. "Shut the fuck up, Billy Billet. Bad egg. Low-life. Fuck-up. Junior, my ass."'

Billy's girlfriend was reading a tabloid. Her eyes were shadowed in aquamarine. Sometimes she looked up and smiled wanly at Billy.

A week later Robert came to the courtroom with a woman. A pretty woman named Denise, but Joel told me she wasn't his wife. We exchanged the briefest of greetings.

The courtroom was muggy. The judge, corpulent and unsentimental. Johnny Barbuto, a bouncer, took the stand.

'Billy came at me with a knife,' Barbuto said. He was burly and thick-necked.

'What can you tell me about the knife?' the judge said. 'Do you know how long the blade was? Did you see the knife?'

'He was going to kill me,' Barbuto said earnestly. 'I sprayed him with dog repellent. Billy said he was blind. Swore a bit. Asked me if I was a tough guy. If I wanted to punch him. If I wanted to do him in.'

'Did you see the knife?' said the judge.

'I heard the knife. The pepper spray affected my vision too.'

'You heard the knife?' The judge laughed and his laughter was an invitation to the courtroom. 'What did you see?'

'I heard the knife drop. Billy bent down to pick up the knife. He wanted to stab me.'

'You're not in the position to say what's in the mind of the accused, Mr Barbuto.'

'He was waiting to get me. He tried to bite off my ear. You can see I'm badly scarred.' Barbuto turned his thick neck.

The judge wiped his forehead. 'Confine your evidence.'

The proceeding went on and on. I was taking notes as fast as I could. I kept writing down testimony as if my life depended on it. But the whole thing was a farce. I could already tell.

Three months later Billy got five years for manslaughter.

Worse than a farce because it wasn't funny. I got it wrong again.

Samuel Beckett said the greatest absurdity is human happiness. I believe that's true.

Joel

The plot thickened. I had Sandra on the line. She was talking through tears.

'Where's Robert? Where in the hell is Robert?' she said. 'I want to know where my husband is.'

I said, 'I'm not playing the boyfriend game. A long time ago I learned never to kiss 'n' tell.'

'I wish I had some fuck-you money to throw at him. To get a divorce.'

'A pretty face like yours. Stop weeping, Sandra. Put down the mop.'

Then for the longest time Jane never brought up Edward's death. It was as if she knew that neither Robert nor I wanted to play ball, so she just left the park. I could see she needed cheering, but I was achy and exhausted.

'If you want, Janie,' I said. 'We could call in the reiki girls for a foot massage. Would you like one of those baby yogurts to calm you down? Should we burn some incense? Cannabis makes you more anxious, right?'

Instead, she was going back to put the finishing touches on her thesis, but she'd been saying that for two or three years.

'Leonardo da Vinci left many things undone,' she said. 'He had so many projects going at once. So many interests. Geology, anatomy, botany, mathematics, painting.'

'Is that true?' I asked.

'Yep. He barely finished a thing. In 1476, he was twice accused of sodomy, but the charges were dismissed because of lack of evidence.'

'You know the damnedest things.'

Jane said, '*Saper vedere*, it's knowing how to see.'

I said, '*Saper vedere* yourself, baby.'

I told her how Philip had started wearing makeup and looking like an old fuddy-duddy queen. And how he wanted to drop acid at eleven in the morning after partying all night.

'Wow,' she said, brightening.

'You're something, Janie. The way you keep up with all my Shakespearean dramas.'

I told her I dreamt I was robbed in the alley where Edward was killed. 'I said, "Look, you can have all my money. Here, take it. Just let me live." And the fuckers ran away.

'What d'ya think, Janie?' She was starting to mope.

She said, 'Can I say something to you?'

'Of course, Janie. Anything, sweet Jane.' And then she started to recite. She said:

> Thou wast not born for death, immortal Bird!
>   No hungry generations tread thee down;
>   The voice I hear this passing night was heard
>   In ancient days by emperor and clown

Can you dig it? She knows this stuff off the top of her head.

I said, 'That's some thousand-petal lotus you got there, Janie. You're just emanating the colour white. Stand by me, kitten, and give me a little shower of that. It's all about rejuvenation, rebirth and joy, isn't it, dah-ling. That's all there is, dontcha know. Up, up and up. Life's a picnic, Jane. You gotta stop laying your blanket on the ant heap?

She looked very depressed, totally *Guernica*. She must suffer from that new millennial dysthymia, the way she casts down her eyes and frowns. But I have a way of tuning her out. I don't even bother to think, oh, she's pathetic and taciturn. Are those real tears in her eyes?

Later, I told her Sting's in town. I may have a shot at doing the hair of Sting.

A little barbershop called the Beauty Dungeon opened up in the alleyway where Edward was killed. You can go there and have your shoes shined for five bucks. Yesterday I had my boots polished. And this guy, very young, very cute, just a kid really, starts licking my boot. He wasn't wearing any underwear and his dick was peeking out of his cutoffs.

'Ahem, ahem,' I said. 'Are you on some kind of subservient trip? Because I've been waiting for you a cigarette and a lifetime.' He had the sweetest face. I wanted to know: 'Am I going to get this treatment on the left side, too?'

He just winked and kept buffing away.

Then I went to Edward's office where this young Asian doctor with a nose ring dressed my boils. She wasn't afraid to touch me anywhere.

I want to participate in the whole movement for wellness.

Robert

Denise had a little black dog Nelson, named after Nelson Mandela, a condominium that overlooked the lake, and a tidy portfolio of mutual funds. In Hollywood she once worked on a script with Martin Scorsese.

'Come and chant the sound of *om* with me,' she said. She was sitting on the floor near the window. 'Then we'll have some champagne and take a bubble bath.'

The trial was over. Sandra wanted me home. She was tired of the back and forth. She wanted me back in the suburbs for good. 'You've got your hot tub,' she said. 'Your barbecue and motorcycle. Not to mention the children. We'd all like to see you more often.'

Denise said, 'I'm not asking you for a cent, Robbie. I don't want any handouts. If you'd like, you're welcome to stay.'

She called me Robbie like my mother, not Robert.

'Do you regret that you never had kids?' I said. 'Are you sorry? Do you feel you missed out?' I was leaving.

'No, Robbie,' she said. 'I think you can do the suffering there for both of us. It serves you right.'

That night Sandra took *Your Child's Self-Esteem* to bed. Then she recited all the calamities that had recently befallen the neighbourhood.

'Five times they had to open Jerry Garver to put the shunt back in,' she said. 'Only seven years old and he was leaking spinal fluid all over the grocery store.'

'Who?' I said. I didn't know what she was talking about. Each time the kids get a cold, Sandra goes out of her mind. She's always thinking up all kinds of hostilities. She won't even let them go down the road on their own.

Then she started to talk about Edward. 'Edward wanted to have sex with me,' she said. 'I never told you. It was after you and I had been going out for a month.'

'I'm not going to ask what happened,' I said. I couldn't even look at her. 'I don't want to know.'

'All the girls loved him. He used to dress so preppie. He was the handsomest boy in the whole school. Did you hear what I said? What's the matter with you? You don't know how lucky you are.'

'About the baby with Down's syndrome? About Jerry Garver and his bike accident? What are you on about now?'

'I know what you're thinking.'

'Let's not forsake Edward's name.'

'You don't even care that he's dead.'

For some reason, I started to think about lying in bed with Jane and discussing the Final Solution. I bet Jane's the type of girl who'd want to do a lot of talking, leave on her undershirt, and turn off the lights. In the morning, she'd serve me orange juice and read my horoscope. I'm a bastard.

Jane

Today I stay in bed, flesh-stainèd finger on my own globèd peony. I give myself the little zing, the burst outside of time, and my mind screams, "Do it!" It's just a thought.

Do what?

It rained all day, it never stopped raining. Upon Keats's gravestone he asked that they write: *Here lies one whose name was writ in water.*

If I don't watch out, I'm going to start hating myself badly again.

I tell myself to calm down, develop a schedule, some predictability, and finish my thesis. Constantly, I say to myself in Italian: *Sono una donna che può finire la thesis.* I am a woman who can finish her thesis.

The Nazis allowed no underclothes in the bunkhouses of Sachsenhausen. The men were not allowed to put their hands under their blankets.

By early 1944, in Buchenwald, the system of pink triangles had broken down, and some prisoners didn't even wear one. Himmler allowed prisoners to be blackmailed into castration. But everyone knew that the kapos had their riding horses, their doll boys.

Keats's mother died of tuberculosis when he was fourteen. He nursed his mother, and he nursed his brother, Tom, who died shortly after Keats began 'Hyperion' in December of 1819. By that time Keats himself had contracted the disease. Within a month or two of his engagement to Fanny Brawne, he was taking laudanum. Some scholars say he died of syphilis.

When the Soviets entered Birkenau, they found 15,400 pounds of women's hair packed into paper bags, hundreds of thousands of shoes, 358,000 men's suits.

The Germans eroticized violence.

When Jewish blood spurts off the knife, that's when you get more kicks from life.

Bettelheim blamed the prisoners of Buchenwald for holding on to their possessions. For not revolting in striped uniforms and berets and wooden shoes. Bettelheim was an ass.

At midnight I wake up; I'm cold. The bedclothes have fallen to the floor.

I think of Joel. His knees hurt. All the medications make his face puffy. Someone stole his new boots when he was passed out on liquid morphine. Then his body flip-flops, diarrhea, constipation. Constipation, diarrhea.

I never heard again from Robert. He must have gone home. He's lucky to have a family. A family must be comforting.

Twenty past one and I still can't sleep. *Where but to think is to be full of sorrow.* Stanza III, 'Ode to a Nightingale', composed around May 1, 1819. The longing of the poet's mind to fuse with the object of imaginative leap.

In October 1944, the Sonderkommando blew up one of four crematoria at Birkenau. Six hundred prisoners escaped. Rosa Robota was accused of supplying dynamite. Before she was hanged, as the trapdoor opened, she shouted, 'Be strong, have courage.'

Courage has glory. In this life we need courage. Hope is good too. So that we can keep up the fight for justice. Maybe forgiveness is stupefaction. I don't know.

After he recovered from a stabbing wound, Beckett went to see his assailant behind bars. He asked him the reason for the assault. The man said, *Je ne sais pas, monsieur.* I don't know.

'I don't know' means confusion and complexity, something very true and deep.

'Not knowing' became the underlying motive for all human action in Beckettian tragedy.

Billy Junior Billet said he didn't like Edward's smile and he didn't like his eyes. Edward Whitby gave him the creeps.

Billy testified that Edward didn't make much noise when he

dragged him off the street and into the alley. Edward fell to the ground and covered his head with his hands. Then there wasn't anything haughty left about him.

What do I feel? I don't think I know what I feel. I'm afraid I don't know how I feel.

Charlotte Delbo wrote that mothers were made to undress in front of their children in the gas chambers at Auschwitz. There was nothing to be done.

At the Passover seder, we recall Rabbi Tarfon, who said, 'The task cannot be completed by you, but neither are you free to desist from the task.' This is the work of *tikkun olam*, repair to the world.

Teach me, O Lord, to number my days. What days? Each day?

The room is dark. A mask hangs over the bed. I could get up and turn on the light. But I'm frightened. Who will I be now?

The End of Metaphors

On a cold, bleak day in late November, Elena hung up a sign in the bookshop window: Closing Sale 60% Off. It was a large white sign with tall black lettering carefully marked out.

'What a terrible sign,' Elena said to Victor.

Without looking at Elena, Victor said, 'Many people are rolling on an ant heap. Being attacked by ants.'

Useless to talk. She returned to her sorting and packing. Books to be sold cheap. Books going back to publishers. Books to be given away to friends. The bookshelves were almost empty. Stacks of books stood in piles on the floor.

Soon no one would remember what had been here. A worn grey carpet, bare white walls, and an old wooden bench, the only designated seating area. And next week the south wall, home to Rhetoric, Poetry and Literary Criticism, would be knocked down for the expansion of the oxygen bar next door.

Theirs had been a stately store. Everyone said so; it was well known in Toronto, expressly for literature. It was called Metaphors and had an elegant plain grey décor. All the walls had been lined by bookshelves. One table for new and noteworthy hardcovers stood near the front. And one table towards the back (in front of Fiction L–M) for Children's Lit. In the last seven years two new shelves were added, devoted to chess and opera, which were Victor's passions.

What happened? First, a year ago, a megabookstore, Wonderment, had opened less than a mile away, and people had flocked to it like homing pigeons. Then ten months of road construction and parking meter installations in front of the store had noisily disrupted both street and pedestrian traffic. Outside jackhammers were still ripping up the street. Finally they had lost their lease to the oxygen bar.

Victor turned books over in his hands, here turning pages, there pausing to read. He may not have eaten breakfast, Elena thought. He was up early, having tossed all night. Before dawn, he'd been reading in bed with a flashlight.

Now he read aloud:

Dear, honoured bookcase, I salute thy existence which for over one hundred years has served the glorious ideals of goodness and justice; thy silent appeal to fruitful endeavour, unflagging in the course of a hundred years, tearfully sustaining through generations of our family, courage and faith in a better future, and fostering in us ideals of goodness and social consciousness.

It was Gayev's tribute to culture and permanence in Act I of *The Cherry Orchard*, Chekhov's last play, the theatrical enactment of dispossession; Elena loved it.

That was the thing about Victor: like a character from Borges he could find the perfect passage.

Ten years ago, when she quit publishing, she had become his partner in the bookstore business he had started ten years before that. She had come to apply for a job and had fallen in love with him immediately. Their courtship revolved mostly around reading each other's favourite books. Victor called writers by their first names and talked about them as if they'd been to dinner the night before. In those days he had waked up Elena in the middle of the night to keep talking. It had been a time of great and quick happiness.

Elena turned away and saw that Angela Larkin, dressed in black, stood at the door, peering in. Angela was a valued customer.

'No,' Angela said, stepping inside. 'Out of business?'

'They are cutting down the cherry orchard,' said Victor. 'I's been sold down da river. I's been run off da land. I's been *un*incorporated.'

'Where will I buy my books? Not from some capitalist pig!' Angela shook out her long red hair from a stylish felt hat. People acted differently around bookshelves. Some flitted, some hopped, some landed. Angela usually made a nose-dive. She was the kind of bibliophile who marked up her books, making copious marginalia. She was totally given to epigrammatic expression. She loved to quote. Last month she had snatched up a collection of Akhmatova's poems from

the front table. She had kissed its cover, not once, but twice, and said,
'"Ay, now am I in Arden."'

'"Wherever they burn books, they will also in the end burn
human beings",' Angela said. Before they could ask, she replied,
'Heinrich Heine.'

Elena winced when she thought of Heine's twisted spine and
'mattress-grave' confinement. Lately she was feeling stiff and arthritic.
It would be better when true winter came and the streets were icy.
Then she'd have an excuse to stay in bed even though she was only
forty. 'No one mentioned anything about burning,' she said. 'Selling
books. Not burning.'

'It *is* a lynching,' said Angela. 'Only now the rope is a retail *chain*.'
This remark gave her a look of clever satisfaction.

Elena said, 'Head office at Wonderment has offered Victor work.'

'How tactless,' Angela said. 'Of course they'd love to have someone knowledgeable. This is sick. Very sick.' Angela was active in city
politics and neighbourhood watch. 'Treating intellect like real estate.
Let's call for a boycott! What did you say?'

Victor dropped to his knees. 'No more song 'n' dance, Mistuh
Man. I's gonna patch my own ole raf.'

Elena glared at Victor. 'For God's sake, Vic, stop it. Get up.' She
had never seen him act so weird and bitter. 'To Victor, "head office" is
a place in the mind.'

Angela looked concerned. 'But what will you *do*? Teach? Travel?
Edit? Write?'

Victor smiled, stood, returned to a book of essays on Armenia.

Yes, Elena wondered, what will I do? She really had no plans,
none whatsoever, not even one. It wouldn't be so easy to find a job.
She *was* worried.

'I hate slogans,' Elena said. 'I hate meetings. More than twenty
people in a room makes me nervous.'

'They should be ashamed,' Angela said. 'Shame on you, Wonderment. Shame on you!' She caught Elena's eye. 'Have you been there?'

Elena was embarrassed to say she had been. She had gone there a
month ago to get a book called *Pain in the Piriformis*. Business was

booming; Wonderment was alien, lit up, garish. There had been fifty copies of a celebrated novel in the display window; Metaphors had ordered two, and never sold them. In his snug-fitting Wonderment vest, the greeter welcomed her, catching her completely off guard. She had smiled automatically, without thinking in response. After a moment of guilt, she had smugly told herself: *He bandied that hello, he doesn't care about me. He'd walk over my dead body. Beware of insincere people who are using you.*

It was true that she was given to exaggeration. Not the same form of hyperbolic antic as Angela, and certainly not Victor's rants of sardonic subversion. Still, the greeter's uniform reminded her of Brownies, a compelling sorority to which she'd never belonged. Wonderment had showy graphics, information stations and steel structures jutting out from the walls. Ten cash registers lined up in a row like slot machines. Pithy aphorisms scrawled across the walls. All those magazines! And the smell of coffee everywhere. It was like some huge municipal installation, a carefully crafted and controlled environment, cross-dressing Las Vegas and Disney World. Admittedly, she saw no gamblers, showgirls or prizefights in Wonderment. And yet on the escalator, she had panicked, and felt tragedy, the way she did on highways and roller coasters and sometimes even in department stores.

That night Elena had some trouble finding her book. She was forced to ask for assistance from a young blond girl who was encumbered by a headset. Elena followed the Wonderment girl, for what seemed like miles, to the Health & Wellbeing section, doggedly trailing the pager that stuck out of her back pocket like a brick. When the girl bent down to peruse a bottom bookshelf, the pager had clunked to the floor with a thud. 'Ha!' Elena said loudly and her back hurt. But she was too proud to sit down in a handy calico armchair. Elena waited, tottered, knowing she was the kind of person who'd be shooed off the vents at closing time. Eventually, the girl found the book and handed it to Elena with a vacant stare. She did not love her bookcase!

Now Angela was hugging a copy of Delmore Schwartz

bagatelles. 'Maybe I'm in search of a mission,' she admitted. 'If I can help you out in any way, let me know.'

In the afternoon, three teenagers wearing headphones came in, who wanted to play checkers. They didn't bother to browse. Another man asked if they had any wrapping paper or greeting cards or candles for sale, and then paused to consider a long row of Anthony Powells. A woman pushing a baby stroller examined what was left of Children's Literature, and asked if Elena thought a beautiful Oxford edition of *The Lady of Shalott* was too eerie for a girl of four.

Victor busied himself in the back room, making telephone calls, and trying to settle accounts.

Later, Mrs Alpert poked her head in. Her wrinkled face was heavily powdered. Old Mr Alpert hung on her arm. In the past, he'd been a solid patron, a prolific reader and purchaser of fine and eclectic poetry collections. In the last years, as his eyesight deteriorated, he'd spent many afternoons talking to Victor and Elena to avoid shopping with his wife.

'Can I drop him off? Same as always,' Mrs Alpert said. 'He doesn't want to walk any more.'

Mr Alpert came in. He leaned his cane up against the wooden bench and sat down. On seeing him, Victor brought forward a fairly new translation of poems by Yannis Ritsos. Then he told Elena he'd meet her at home later and he went out to the bank.

'I'm sorry,' Mr Alpert said. He held the book in his lap. 'Even the large print's too small for me.'

Elena sat down next to him on the bench. 'Would you like me to read you something?'

'Mind if I talk instead?'

He had visited his youngest daughter that morning in the loony bin, he said. He spoke of her as a Cordelia. He said she was the princess of Seven-South. All she wanted to do was read.

'Last summer she read all of Shakespeare, Cervantes and Gogol,' Mr Alpert said. 'A brilliant mind. So much intelligence. First calibre.'

'Imagine.'

'Of course it's hard for her to find employment. Too shy to teach. Easily bored. Not one for the out-of-doors. And office situations are intolerable.' He patted the book of poems. 'Maybe she's better off where she is.'

'Do you think so? I don't know, Mr Alpert. I'm not sure what I'll do. I'm not trained for much either.'

'What a racket!' Mr Alpert's filmy eyes shot to the ceiling.

Elena got up and went to a pile of books.

After a while, Mr Alpert shouted, 'So you're packing up!'

'Yes,' Elena shouted back. 'We've been leased to the oxygen bar next door.'

'I like a good stiff drink.'

'Oh, they don't sell liquor. It's not that kind of bar.'

'What do they sell?'

'Air. Rarefied oxygen.'

'Bunk.' Mr Alpert snorted and then he sat quietly; the book of Ritsos' poems trembled in his hands.

Soon Mrs Alpert rapped on the door. Her net bags were filled with fruit. She waved a packet of strawberries. 'Two ninety-nine. From Chile. Dirt cheap.'

Elena helped Mr Alpert to his feet. 'I suppose you won't be here next week,' he said.

'No. We'll miss you.' Elena promised to keep in touch.

'Sometimes I give my daughter a monetary gift. My wife calls it a reward. But it's nothing of the sort. Can I offer you and Victor a little something?'

'Thank you,' Elena said. 'We'll be all right.' She paused. 'You're a kind man, Mr Alpert. I really don't know what to say.'

At five Elena turned off the lights and locked the door behind her. Out on the street she stood between two steel poles and a gate of wire fencing. She paused in front of the oxygen bar and looked inside. The room was dimly lit, cast in a dusky purplish fog, and lamps hung from the ceiling like intravenous bags. Sitting at the bar, chatting and drinking bottled juice, were about a dozen people who wore the apparatus of the sickly no longer able to breathe on their own. Thin tubes ran up their noses, around their heads, down their chests. Off to one side of the bar a man in a reclining chair adjusted his tubes with slow steady concentration. He raised his hooded eyes when he saw Elena staring at him like a ghost in a sepulcher. He beckoned insipidly. *Come in.*

Shyly Elena shook her head, and took a deep breath of the cold evening air as if it were clean and good and free, and coughed. Her lungs felt squashed. She stepped back on the sidewalk in front of Metaphors. It already looked empty, dark, deserted. She pressed her face up against the window. The closing sign completely obliterated her view. She couldn't make out a thing.

Later over dinner she would describe this scene to Victor as precisely as she could. She'd employ the language of metaphor in an effort to explain her feelings at this moment. I was a naked bride, she'd say, a weary traveller, a pomegranate seed, a forgotten sailor awaiting news from home. Because that was the way she and Victor talked with each other and found meaning. She'd tell him how she hit the window once with the palm of her hand, not hard, and then turned away when she realized that this part of her life was over for good. Wondering what to do with her sadness, she walked along, thinking of books.

About Glennie

Glennie Ambrose paused on the steps of the university theatre, reminding herself not to walk onto the stage and blather some cheap, dime-store confession of love. It was a bright day, clear and crisp, but sombre clouds moved in Glennie's head, quite unaffected by the late October sun.

Inside the theatre, Tucker McCarthy, who had flown in from New York to direct his new play, *The DNA Quest,* paced up and down in front of Lydia Marquette. Lydia, like Glennie, was vying for the part of the girlfriend of the murderer's son. Also on stage, in a striped stocking cap, was Richard Furry, an old friend of Glennie's from drama school days. Richard, a part-time window dresser, was a master of disguises. He loved to dress up. Glennie took a seat in the last row and shrugged off her coat.

'C'mon, c'mon. It all rests on a fingerprint. Let's hear it again,' said Tucker. 'Hard and fast. I want it quick. Quick. Like Mamet.'

In her flat voice, Lydia began to say her lines. *'I live in the hollow,'* she said. *'Love is the scar on my bones.'*

Isn't it strange, isn't it strange, Glennie told herself, as the words of Tucker McCarthy reverberated against the walls, how well I understand Tucker's suffering. She had loved him for two years. Since the summer he had come to conduct a seven-day workshop on a cycle of his mystery plays: *The Twitching Eyebrow, The Muscle of Disaster* and his thriller, *A Gesture of Remorse.* No one had ever before aroused such passion in Glennie, had taught her so much in such a short time.

What a singularly intense, funny, brilliant man was Tucker McCarthy. No one could write about the nuances of lost love like Tucker; the ache and yearning of his characters was almost unbearable. How he understood the power of language and the pitfalls of fate. When the week was over and it was time for everyone to resume their so-called normal lives, Glennie could do nothing but wait until the time she might see him again. Her heart was half of what it had been, like a leftover sandwich, wrapped up in plastic, placed at the back of the fridge. For its lessons on patience, she reread *War and Peace*.

Glennie was not conventionally beautiful in the Hollywood sense, but she was pretty enough, if you liked, say, a Modigliani type with freckles. She knew something of Tucker McCarthy's reputation as a womanizer, and feared that he might have concocted a perception of her as a woman of limited sexual experience, which was not far from the truth. She hoped this would not eventually cause him to reject her, if and when they ultimately got together, which she sincerely believed might happen. Although she had never married, she was not a virgin by any means.

Since she had fallen in love with Tucker, she had seriously wondered if she had ever known true intimacy. In fact, when Glennie's last boyfriend, an accountant, had moved in with her, she had taken a job almost immediately in a summer stock musical revue at a resort hotel several hundred miles north of Toronto. Never had she been as happy as she was in her little cabin by the peaceful lake. The old Broadway show tunes (she loved to sing and dance) had proven to be a great vehicle for her talent. A rigorous schedule of rehearsals and performances had left her with barely the time to consider what was going on back in the city. By September, her boyfriend was seeing another woman whom he eventually married and they had recently gone to China to adopt a baby.

Indeed, her love for Tucker McCarthy hadn't been quite immediate, because she had warned herself thoroughly about the possibility of falling for someone in a position of authority, someone who regardless of feeling, or mutual attraction, must necessarily maintain a professional distance by virtue of ethics and position. In the beginning, she hadn't even understood what was happening. At first, affection suffused her like the sweet perfume of summer flowers. Then desire seeped in with a more debilitating humidity.

'*My eyes, my eyes,*' Richard was shouting. '*Bespattered! Wounded! I've lost my peripheral vision!*'

'So the fortune teller tells him,' Tucker said, 'that he's been in the slow lane, tuttle-tuttle-tuttle, and it's time to move into express. This isn't some gypsy reading his tarot cards. No Madame Zara with balloons, long earrings and the Hanging Man tucked up her sleeve. She's a psychic princess living in the suburbs. She points to a bulge on his knuckles and says, "Listen, Freddy, how about a little migraine if you don't change your tune? How about a stroke or *cancer?*"'

'Got it,' said Richard. Tufts of blond hair winged out from his cap.

'Leave your manners at the door, Dick,' said Tucker. 'Forget your breeding. Down to the sewer you go. Poor Freddy. Watching a Cheerios commercial while his father stabbed his pregnant mother forty times. Ever since he's been verbal, he's defended the old man. But lately Freddy just happens to get these pictures in his mind of his father wielding a knife.'

Tucker began to kick wildly at an old cardboard box on the stage that was supposed to represent a coffin. It reminded Glennie of the sheet-covered piano that stood at centre stage in the third act of Tucker's *The Tipping Ladder*. She now got up from her seat and began to make her way down the middle aisle.

'Freddy's hopped up on Dexedrine,' Tucker went on. 'Slightly crazed and incoherent. And now he knows his old man's dangerous. He killed his mother in cold blood. And he'd probably kill Freddy. Here we are at the grave of his mother. A bunch of forensic types are about to exhume the body. And all of a sudden Freddy remembers something happy from his childhood. When his social worker took him to a pet store and he heard a parrot squawk.'

Tucker grabbed Richard's shirtsleeve.

'Say it, Dick. Say it now like the parrot's on your shoulder. Say it like a seizure. You're surrounded by air, but you can't get at it. C'mon now, Dickie, we're opening up the coffin and removing the shroud. Give me those parrot words. Like Doctor Faustus.'

'*Willy nilly,*' said Richard as if he were suffocating. '*Willy nilly.*'

With those words, a leak was sprung, a fountain opened. Glennie thought she might faint or explode. Last night she had been unable to sleep, again and again going over this scene by the grave in her mind.

The murderer's son and his girlfriend. But all along she was writing a new script in which the audition was finished and she invited Tucker back to her apartment. She would light candles. 'Come, come sit down and I'll make you a cup of tea. Dear man, you're worn out,' she would say, and begin to tell him about herself. 'My father was largely absent during my girlhood ... Even though Mother worked, she was always beholden to him.

'Are you sure you're interested in all this?' she would interrupt herself, knowing full well that he was. And then if she served cognac or wine, her gestures and conversation would quicken. 'Of course there was damage ... complete and ruthless damage ... in all the old pictures the whole family looks stunned ... My first winter I had a high fever and Mother didn't know if I would live or die ... And I'm the one child who bears my father's name.'

Glennie would have to admit that her job at a manufacturing firm was boring and clerical. 'And then the photocopier broke down and we all stood around as if it were an altar,' she would say to amuse him. 'No one knew whether to laugh or to cry.'

Then Tucker became her lover. She even called him Tuck or Tuck-a-long. Finally, she would take him in her arms and tell him that her love was cellular, embedded in her marrow, circulating through her blood. If he were willing to stay for dinner she would make him her favourite recipe of Colette's roast chicken with thirty garlics.

Now Glennie was on stage. Tucker was trying to warm her up. His face was exactly as she remembered, boyish, pale, smooth.

'Freddy's girlfriend,' he was saying, 'is a very sensitive type. Everything affects her. Starving peasants. Limping dogs. She's a real crusader.'

What am I doing here? Glennie asked herself. It was like her mother begging her father for grocery money. McCarthy would never give her the part. And she was afraid he would be able to read her mind.

'What is the girlfriend's reality?' Tucker now said. 'A mist through which she pretends to cavort. A narrow vista through the trees. All along she's believed in the father's innocence. For Freddy's sake.'

'Okay,' said Glennie.

'Take it easy,' said Tucker. 'No sirens or alarms. Just say the words. Like Ibsen's *Ghosts*.'

Behind the dark velvet curtains Glennie flailed around until she found the heavy door marked EXIT. Out on the fire escape she was shaking and her throat burned. If he gave the part to Lydia, then she'd just have to find another role for herself. And if not in a play, then on a TV show, in a goddamn sitcom. What did she care? Her mind swam from one possibility to the next – widow, mother, sister, friend, a woman everything, cook, secretary, maid and nurse. And yet there was always a chasm – the character failed to evacuate, threw herself from a bridge, cut off her hands and stood there smiling. Only to emerge as a waif or a goddess of salt.

When Glennie finally fell asleep, she dreamed of climbing the winding staircase (an image McCarthy freely borrowed from Yeats) to her voice lesson. And who had opened the door at the top of the stairwell ... whose head bobbed out? Not her singing coach, Mrs Glückstein ... not Tucker McCarthy ... b-b-b-but Monica Lewinsky! *Monica*, Glennie had whispered, almost choking in her dream. *Is that really you?*

When she woke up, Glennie could hardly believe it herself. Then she cried from loneliness. She thought she might die from loneliness, though it had yet to kill her. There must have been a part of her that was certain that Tucker loved her too. How she had fanned that little ember to keep it alive. Did she have a great or trivial imagination? Hadn't he taken her hand on the last night of the workshop when everyone was outside on the grass playing Costumes in a Box? Hadn't he murmured, 'Your eyes are the colour of heather'?

He had made her feel so English countryside, so weathered barn-wood. The night had been moonlit. The smell of freesia and roses, intoxicating.

Would she, Glennie, just keep loving him on and on? The tears she had shed for Tucker McCarthy: only God knew. But she mustn't let him see her unhappiness: what an old-fashioned way to attract attention. And yet she wasn't so young any more. She now wore reading glasses and had psoriasis on her elbows. Thank goodness those days when a self-respecting woman could throw herself on a man's mercy were long over.

The others had come out and crowded onto the fire escape landing to smoke cigarettes and admire the weather. 'Not a cloud in the sky,' said Richard.

Tucker gazed out over the campus as if onto the waves of a crashing, black sea.

'I feel Titanic,' said Lydia, looking at him. 'Absolutely Titanic.'

Glennie craned her long neck to cast herself into Tucker's line of vision. She waved one hand in front of his face like a semaphore. Ahoy, but he was far off. She could find no island of comfort there. She sighed in frustration. Must she remain a bumptious understudy, always lagging behind while the true meaning of a dramatic event unfolded?

Glennie couldn't go on like this another year, another month, another day or hour. No, she must tell him. One more minute and she'd never sleep another night. Surely he must know.

She approached him and he said pleasantly, 'How ya been, Glennie?'

'Fine, fine,' she said. 'Fine.'

'Did I get you worked up in there?'

'Oh, I suppose. A little.'

Then Glennie propelled herself against Tucker's chest with such force that he slipped on the iron grating. She grabbed his hand and his cigarette tripped from his fingers. In an instant she had him pinned precipitously over the railing. A brief struggle ensued in the shining autumn light as Tucker struggled to capture his footing.

'Man overboard,' said Richard.

'Glennie's doing vaudeville,' said Lydia.

'Willy nilly,' said Tucker. 'Are you trying to kill me?' With his free hand he kept trying to shove Glennie away.

So Glennie let go. Then she remembered the words that only last night she had tried unsuccessfully to commit to memory. They bubbled up from deep inside her. She spoke:

Dig up the earth and make me a bed. Cradle me. Why do you wait to undo?
Truth is etched in the body. Haul up the ruse of doubtful ends. Twist of night.
Logic's braid. Double helix of the soul's dark past. You live!

'Good stuff!' said Richard.

'That was some hug,' Tucker said fondly. Lydia laced her arm
through his and he patted her hand.

Again Glennie catapulted forward, zigzagging down the fire
escape on the tips of her toes. By the time she reached the bottom of
the stairs she had broken into song. On a hill of golden leaves she
pirouetted, her head full of strange new feelings. It was time to change
her life. How?

The Hanukkah Gift

Last night was the Hanukkah party.

In the morning Danny's mother called to say that Danny needed to stay near me, that's what his therapist said, after all I'm his teacher. 'He gets strength and security from your presence,' she told me. 'Open spaces like the gym leave him without a container for his feelings. He carved a hole in the bus seat last week. Next time, he could carve a hole in me. Try.'

It was late November, a general lessening of light. JFK conspiracy theories on the radio. I had been drinking my coffee. Was it a drastic oversimplification or could I blame TV and magazines for why I never felt at home in my body?

I had been thinking a Jewish girl like me used to be called zaftig, and there was nothing wrong with having hips and breasts and thighs. I was thinking of Ruth Handler, the daughter of Polish Jewish immigrants, who invented the Barbie doll. Hardly anyone ever calls me Barbie, even though my name is Barbara.

In Hawaii, I had heard that obesity was tolerated. If you go into a restaurant, the waiter will bring you two chairs. Maybe not on Maui, but on some of the other islands.

I had started telling myself jokes. Like, do you know what happens if a fat person stops eating? He starves. Ha ha. And, do you know why men don't get mad cow disease? Because they're pigs, ha ha. Ha, *ha*.

The teasing from the boys was the worst. You have a pretty face came later from my girlfriends and always from my mother.

I was worrying where I would be when the Prozac wore off because I'd gained twenty extra pounds on Prozac. I was thinking all I want is to be loved by that special someone. I was saying to myself I'd rather be a thin cow than a fat cow in Pharaoh's dream.

At the school Danny was waiting for me and he said, 'Let me tell you a joke.'

'Okay, but hurry up, you have to help me get ready for the Hanukkah party.'

Danny told a joke about a boy named Trouble and his brother, Shutup. 'Trouble got lost, so Shutup went to look for him. A policeman asked, What's your name? So Shutup said, Shutup. The policeman said, Are you looking for trouble? And Shutup said, How did you know?'

A great punchline. A good joke.

Sometimes I think I'll quit therapy and become an alcoholic.

I went over the story of Hanukkah with the kids. I wanted to make sure they got it right. And a king rose up and called himself Antiochus Epiphanes, which means the visible god. But the people called him Antiochus 'Epimanes' because he was a madman. He prohibited the Jews from Sabbath observance: he even put a statue of Jupiter (which bore his likeness) on the altar in the Holy Temple. And the pig, the animal most *abhorred* by the Jews, was brought in to be sacrificed.

The kids sang, 'See me. Light me. Watch me. Bless me,' to the tune of *Tommy*'s 'Listening to You'. The parents loved it. Simon the storyteller did something with puppets. The mothers passed out dreidels and chocolate money. The music began. I was standing by the food tables, when Simon came over and said, 'I'm having one more latke. Did you have a taste?'

'I've had several,' I said.

The band was playing the hora. Simon took my hand and we were running, one foot in front, one foot behind, kick right, kick left, run, clap, run. My breasts were flopping. I threw back my head.

'It's a party in the gym,' I called to Simon above the music.

'It's Vest Side Story,' Simon called back.

Later we had a few more latkes and some tabouleh, which was very good. He told me he was going to Cuba. 'Havana Gila,' he laughed. 'Get it?'

He's funny, I thought. I like a man with a sense of humour, and his looks aren't bad either. He's older than I am and he's been married, but so what?

No one was listening to the rabbi. He was up there on stage looking a little humiliated. 'Hanukkah is not only a children's story,' he said. 'Antiochus, Haman, Chmielnicki, Hitler, Ferdinand, Stalin, Saddam Hussein! There was always a madman out to assail us. For what reason? Parents, can you quiet your children? Maybe if you take away the dreidels, just until I'm finished.

'Year after year we're singing the same songs. Year after year we're lighting the candles. Yes, there was a military victory, but only one jar of oil was found in the Temple. The oil should have lasted eight days, but how many days did it burn?'

'EIGHT DAYS!' yelled the children.

'Not by force, but by spirit,' said the rabbi. 'Sh, sh, sh. So why do we celebrate Hanukkah?'

'Because we get PRESENTS', shouted Rebecca Weinberg, a beautiful child, extremely intelligent.

Simon was telling me about his ex-wife, an installation artist. 'In her last exhibit, she covered an entire room in a block print of ashes, in what she called a swastika/sauvastika motif. It covered all four walls.'

'What's a sauvastika?' I asked.

'An inverted swastika. Supposedly the sauvastika was a life symbol before the Nazis got hold of it. Ash is carbon. A basic life compound. The whole space was filled. It was heavy. Oppressive.'

'I bet,' I said. 'I see.'

'Thanks for listening to this,' Simon said. 'I've been very pent up. My wife's the daughter of survivors. Of course I understood her work intellectually. But I used to leave the gallery dreaming of Monet's water lilies. When I bought a mango shake at Juice for Life, I felt guilty. She called me a coward.'

'It sounds like you miss her very much,' I said.

Suddenly the room, the entire gym, went completely black. Pandemonium!

'Where are the lights?' someone shouted. 'Turn on the lights! Does anyone know where the lights are in this room?'

'Who has a match?' yelled another. 'Get a flashlight!'

The children squealed.

Rebecca hissed, 'Danny!'

'Danny,' his mother called. 'Danny, where are you? DANIEL!'

Then I was touched on my shoulders. Someone pulled me forward. I was kissed very gently, very lightly, very sweet. Immediately a ripple of sensation that I hadn't felt in many years.

When the lights went on, I was standing alone. Danny's mother had him by the elbow and was roughly leading him from the gym. Simon was by the stage. He didn't even look at me.

'Light the Hanukkah *licht lach*, for God's sake,' said Natie Silver's grandfather. 'For God's sake, light the menorahs.'

You can say what you want. A life of irony. The fire truck burns. You can say he kissed me in the dark. A kiss is still a wonderful thing. Chekhov wrote about a kiss and so did Turgenev. You can say Simon had no right to do it, and I would agree, the evil patriarchy, blah, blah, *blah*. But for a brief moment, my soul lifted up.

Acknowledgements

For a thousand helping hands along the way, I would like to extend my heartfelt gratitude to Mary Jo Morris, Tim O'Brien, Nino Ricci, Josef Skvorecky and Joe Kertes, and to my friends Karen Bamford, Marie Bamford (all the Bamfords: Mr and Mrs, Susan, Joy, Denise, Jim, partners and children, et al.), Theresa Byrne, Kathleen Conway, Carolyn Tanner, Paula Markus, Judy Shier Weisberg, Robert Cupido, Denis Pelletier, Curt Peoples, Sarah Pettersen, Virginia Kelly, Cindy Lichtman, Bev and Joel Lehman, Barbara Rabinowitz, Pam Silver, Marta Davni, and Ramonda Talkie. I am grateful to you one and all.

I would also like to thank everyone at The Porcupine's Quill, especially Jack Illingworth, Doris Cowan, and of course, Tim and Elke Inkster.

Special thanks and appreciation go to John Metcalf, writer, editor and national treasure.

Some of the stories in this collection were originally published in slightly different form in the following: *Grain*: 'Too Much to Tell'; *Prairie Fire*: 'The Middle of the Triangle'; *The Antigonish Review*: 'Dear Natalie'; *The Canadian Jewish News*: 'The Hanukkah Gift'; *The New Quarterly*: 'Love Junk' and 'Snap'; *The Fiddlehead*: 'Home for Lunch'.

Joan Alexander was born in Chicago, and moved to Canada in 1979, where she worked as a teacher and a journalist for many years while continuing to study the writing craft. Her work has appeared in a number of Canadian literary journals and has been nominated for the Journey Prize, a National Magazine Award and *Best New American Voices*. She lives in Toronto, in the Bathurst and Eglinton area, and is currently working on a novel: *Lost Boy: Intermittent Rewards for Valiant Souls*.